TRADING FOURS

A Novel

ANGELA CAROLE BROWN

HAIKU HOUSE

Published by Haiku House
U.S. Copyright Registration No. TX 6-194-143
ISBN-13: 978-0615798622

Book Jacket Design by Angela Carole Brown
Author Photograph by Jim Henken
Visit the author at: **www.angelacarolebrown.com**

Printed in the United States of America

To my fellow musicians, who have provided me with wonderful stories throughout the years, from which I have culled to create this tale, and without whose presence my life would be the poorer.

TRADING
FOURS

"Damn it all blues,
screwed to the melting frozen walk of
dared-to-embrace stone,
concrete hard, imagined soft"
—— *Charles Mingus, "Beneath the Underdog"*

"In a world of casuals, no one can hear you scream."
—— *Roy Wiegand III,*
October 6, 2001
Bedrossian Wedding

Every human being who has ever called himself a musician has, at some point in his life, picked up an instrument and dreamed of legend.

It is a dream that for some surely includes preferred seating at waiting-list-only restaurants, VIP standing at the plushest five-star hotels, entourages of body guards and screaming fans, and riders with every demand that royalty is allowed. All the luscious, decadent clichés.

More profoundly, it is a dream of that moment on stage. Coltrane had it. Jimi had it. When through the sheer weight and breadth of their gift, their ability to compel, even change thought, they manage to place an audience under some kind of inexplicable spell, and in doing so, shift culture just ever so slightly.

And it is only the opinion of this scribbler, but that is, without a doubt, the true dream.

The reality, more often than not, is just a tiny variation on that theme:

"And now ladies and gentlemen! Please welcome, for the first time ever as husband and wife, Mister and Missus Joel and Rebecca Cohen! Let's hear it for them, Ladies and gentlemen! A-one, a-two, a-one, two, three, four…"

That's a casual.

In musician parlance, it means a private party. A birthday bash, a wedding reception, an office mixer, a bar mitzvah; the list goes on. New York musicians call them *club dates*. There are probably a half dozen terms for it in a half dozen cities. *Casual* is the L.A. term.

According to *Webster's Encyclopedic Unabridged Dictionary*, the word casual means: 1. occurring by chance. 2. without definite or serious intention. 3. seeming or tending to be *indifferent, apathetic, blasé.*

Ironic (telling? hilarious? tragic?) that such a word would even have been adapted to refer to the making of music.

The question that begs examination, of course, is: What happens to the person who chooses a path that embeds from the very start the implicit suggestion of its non-impact, its barely-holding-on-to significance, its indifferent, apathetic, blasé place in the world?

The answer? No one chooses to become a casual musician.

It chooses him. By means equally desperate and rationalizing:

"Hey, it's a nobler living than phone sex or selling used cars."

TRISTAN

For the new Mr. and Mrs. Joel Cohen, this is the happiest, loveliest, most romantic, straight-out-of-a-movie moment in their lives. A moment they will remember forever. For Tristan Baylor, the gig's leader, it is that exact same moment two hundred days out of the year. Just another casual. Or bloodbath, depending on his mood. Another chance to hear the chick singer next to him (whose name he doesn't bother to remember) screech out a too-high-for-her-range rendition of Andrew Lloyd Webber, and screw up the form, and over-riff with her vocal acrobatics, which Tristan can invariably count on from most of the chick singers he works with. Their only use, as far as he is bitterly concerned, is to blow him in the back of his SUV after the gigs.

As he entertains loathings that have surely become routine, but with a smile on his face to show he cares about making the Cohens's special day even more special, Mr. and Mrs. Newly Married are in Heaven, dancing the choreographed routine they've worked on, with the record, at home.

It had been their first dance, which they are now reprising, choreography and all, as their last dance of the evening.

Thank God this shit is over.

When the singer comes to the close of her Broadway show tune medley, Tristan notes to himself that for every song she sings badly, she will owe him a blow job. And he'll be more than happy to owe her one back if she ever Just once sings a song in tune, proper form, actual melody, something! for fuck's sake. She is a Christina Aguilera wannabe who has no clue what it takes to be a musician, and who saturates every song she sings with all of her little R&B chick licks, whether it is the appropriate style or not.

But lest anyone thinks this is just a chick thing, Tristan rationalizes, as he finds himself defending his silent rant against imaginary complaints on his misogyny, which even Tristan has to cop to, the truth is that there are guys on this bandstand, as well, who have no business being paid good money to pluck, strike, blow, or whatever various sodomies they perform on those poor instruments. Yet here they are; guys who can officially call themselves professionals, because they have the 1099's at the end of the tax year to prove it.

To Tristan's bored chagrin, this blessed event has made no promises to give him any reason to actually stay awake. He's heard so many wild stories over the years, usually around the break room roundtables at gigs, about outrageous incidents that happened at this or that wedding reception. Like the one about the bridegroom who gets up during the reception to give a toast. He proceeds to tell the guests to please look under each of their seats, where they will find a little something from the bridal party…to them…with love. And he dedicates that gesture to his new bride and his best man. What the guests find under their seats is a Polaroid of same bride performing a gifted fellatio on same best man, apparently snapped by a private investigator, hired by the suspicious groom, on the night before.

That particular tale has been floating around for years, with no one guy actually able to claim it any longer as his own, and which is considered casual legend.

Or the time that the groom's mother popped the bride in the jaw, careening her, white gown, bloody nose, and all, into the six-tiered cake. Apparently, icing rained down on all the instruments, causing various electrical shorts and other brilliant mayhem.

But Tristan isn't so lucky this evening. No such

mischievous, diary-warranting fun will happen tonight. Everything has gone smoothly and without a hitch, due to caterers, florists, and coordinators doing their jobs efficiently; and largely, as well, because of Tristan's expertise as a bandleader. And the bride and groom won't ever even realize his value in making their evening seamless, because to them he is just the faceless, nameless tuxedo behind the microphone and guitar. And Tristan will go home at the end of this night, as he does every night, with the requisite back pains from all the equipment hauling, and virtually unappreciated for his efforts.

It doesn't help that he doesn't even especially like half the guys in his band this evening. Not them as people, necessarily. Just their playing. The reason is because in the casual world musicians don't largely book their own personnel. They are assembled by a music contractor, that dubious necessity that musicians in this town have come to count on, if they want to make a living. There's never a "band." Just freelance players, showing up and seeing who else they're playing with that night.

Now, this doesn't automatically assume that terrible music is guaranteed to be made. There have been extraordinary moments when sheer magic has been created between total strangers. If you're a good musician, that can happen.

But not tonight.

Tonight, he's got Lance Mitchell, the diehard jazzer tenor player, who loves blowing his bebop licks over *Heard It Through the Grapevine*. Some chick he hopes never to gig with again, who is looking to be the next Beyoncé. And a keyboard player, who has to open a book for every tune called, instead of just having them under his belt, so that things can segue quickly and smoothly. They are all decent musicians. For the most part. Even if each one nurses his/her little individual quirks on the bandstand. And even if they aren't all necessarily the right choices for tonight's agenda.

A bebopper on a rock/R&B gig? What are you people thinking?

This is what you often get with a contracted band. There are some fifty-odd contractors in town, but only a handful who actually have the significant, predominantly wealthy Beverly Hills accounts, which, in Los Angeles, is the community that almost single-handedly keeps musicians employed.

Tristan works for one of the largest outfits, Fortune Music Events, and has since the late seventies. He knows every musician in the office stable. But lately the personnel has begun shifting. Old guys leaving, new guys coming in. Some of the best musicians are being replaced by dreck, because it is more cost-effective, and Tristan is beginning to wonder how much longer he'll last, either before he gets fed up with it all, or they get fed up with him and his increasing malaise on the bandstand.

Tristan Baylor has officially begun his trek down that apprentice's road of the spirit-depleted. This job has beaten his back for thirty long years. And he sees no real end in sight. He just isn't sure, any longer, what untactful thing he might be capable of if he has to hear a screeching rendition of *I Will Survive* one more time. Or count off *The Stripper*, so that the groom can pull the garter off his bride's leg with his teeth. Or count the bride in for her bouquet toss, so that she can fake the throw first, laughing cleverly, as though she is the first bride in the history of man to have ever done that. Or invite the father-of-the-bride up with his daughter for the father/daughter dance, to *Butterfly Kisses*. Or bear the mother-of-the-bride, a truly unique species of human, screaming in his ear because the band's too loud, or not loud enough, or playing all the wrong songs. And goddamn it, she's paid good money for this!

It is his job to make sure every bit of protocol gets taken care of on schedule. It is his job to count off tunes, and make sure they are appropriate for the moment. It is his job to play referee between a bride who's screaming for more rock & roll and a mother-of-the-bride who wants more society music for the older folks to dance to. It is his job not to piss off the food captain by throwing him off his schedule, because the band played the wrong kind of song and got the guests up dancing when they should be eating, or sitting bored when they should be cutting a rug. It is his job to be charming and witty and personable, as he recites silly patter that he now knows in his sleep, like:

"Ladies and gentlemen, the bride and groom invite you to join them on the dance floor for their first dance…"

Here's the cutesy little line to use with a stubborn crowd.

"…come on, ladies and gentlemen. Legend has it that for every couple that joins them on the dance floor, the bride and groom will add another year of connubial bliss to their marriage calendar. You don't want it to be said that you were the one responsible for their divorce." *Hah-hah-hah-hah, blah-blah-blah, yuck-yuck-yuck-suck-FUCK!* And if he has to say that stupid line one more time…

It is his job to be referee, juggler, and magician, all in one. And oh yeah…it's also his job to be a good musician.

There are times when it's easy to forget that little detail.

"Thank you, ladies and gentlemen," Tristan says over the microphone, but is abruptly interrupted by a tipsy bride.

"Can you please play just one more song?" she begs, with more amorousness in her gestures than should be coming from a newly married woman. Never mind that she made it perfectly and maniacally clear earlier that the first dance was to be reprieved as the last dance, and which they have just reprieved and have come to the close of the evening.

"Please, please, please, please, please!" she slobbers, as the groom stumbles off to his table of drunken buddies.

Technically, Tristan can't really refuse her, because they are still on the clock. They all thought for a moment, like an evil prick tease, that they were closing this thing out early. *There's barely anyone left!* Now the bride is begging for one more.

"I wanna go out with a bang, not a whimper. Play somethin' up, hard rockin'. Somethin'! Whooooop!"

She is already starting to party to the song in her head. With a smile that barely masks a grimace, Tristan has the drummer count off *Play That Funky Music, White Boy,* while he kicks into a syncopated rhythm guitar that is funkier than most White boys out there. He has the kind of singing voice that can never carry a jazz standard with much finesse, but is rough around the edges in the best sense of the word. And with it, he has often pulled off the most electrifying renditions of tired old casual regulars.

Meanwhile, he is also the loudest guitar player that most of these wedding guests have ever heard. He is loud even to the band. They often tease him. And this time, during an intense Jimi-esque solo, Lance puts down his saxophone, takes off his tux jacket, and throws it over Tristan's amp, to muffle it just ever so slightly.

It's all just meant to be a joke, of course, and Tristan and Lance are great friends, but Tristan doesn't have much of a sense of humor about his loudness. He will always claim that he is just appropriately loud for the occasion, and that he knows when it's time to be mellower, thank you!

The truth is, Tristan Baylor is slowly losing his hearing. It happens to all music war-horses. And honestly, he can never really tell if he's too loud. It sounds perfectly bearable to him. Of course, for rock & roll and funk, loud is definitely the order of business. But every so often he'll notice party guests cringing their faces or holding their ears, and Tristan will usually just roll his eyes and continue giving them his brilliance, albeit voluminous.

And that's just it. Tristan Baylor is brilliant. Or at least inspired. He has the respect of the rest of the office. Every musician in the stable has nothing but glowing things to say about him as a player, as well as a leader. He can cop the Pat

Martino thing in one tune and wipe Jeff Beck off the map in another, with equal finesse.

And just as his guitar is about to explode during his solo on *White Boy*, he kicks into the lick — that famous lick — from Hendrix's *Purple Haze*. The band goes wild, even if the audience isn't especially clued in to the sheer visceral energy on stage. They dance with lamp shades on their heads and drunken slurs on their lips. But Tristan is lighting a fire in the rest of the band, who follow him willingly into Hendrixland. The singer even starts thrashing her head up and down, and "woooooo"ing all over the place. Even though for most of the evening she's been just a little perturbed that Tristan's been hogging all the songs.

And once he finishes a round of Hendrix, he yells, "break it down!" and everything falls to a quiet, steady beating of the drums, as he goes right back to a verse of *White Boy*. By the time they reach the out-chorus for one last round, it's cooking all over again.

By the time the night is finally over, the band has given the wedding guests its all, to make Mr. and Mrs. Cohen's night perfect. They appropriately mellowed things out for the cocktail hour and dinner set, with the likes of Jobim and Ellington and Cole Porter, danced them until they were stupid tired with doses of Motown, rock, and disco. They honored every stumbling, drunken request from uncles and sisters and best friends since high school, who brought up every bright idea from ABBA to Lynyrd Skynyrd, and, of course, the requisite joke-request that is as old and as tired as the back alley skank, *"Freebird!"* They bore up the high anxiety of the bride's mother, and are managing to bleed ear-splittingly into the night's oblivion, until Tristan, in DJ voice, finally bids the happy couple many years of wedded bliss, and signs off with the signature, "see you all at the ten-year anniversary. From Fortune Music. Good night, everybody."

Guys are unplugged, wrapping cords, shoving instruments in their various cases, and undoing their bow ties before Tristan has even finished uttering good night. This is the part of the evening when Tristan packs up his gear with a silence that does its best to drown out remembrances of Aretha Franklin's *Respect* and Kool & the Gang's *Celebration*; when he tries to remember what he's here for and entertains a kind of pensive reflection. But guys invariably try to chat and buzz and stir with him about the food they got fed, or how hilarious the best man's toast was, or the asshole food captain they all hate at this particular hotel, or the shitty load-in through a scummy loading dock, down work corridors, and through laundry rooms and kitchens. It is such a buzz in Tristan's ear. He just wants to quietly tear down his speakers and his amp and his monitors, and wrap his pile of cords, and pack up the horn charts, and fold up his music stand. But he isn't a jerk, so he'll have to smile and laugh through their various bitches and save solitude for the ride home. Tristan has bitches, too. But lately, they seem to run so much deeper than whether he was allowed to get his hands on a dinner roll from the kitchen without getting said hand slapped.

Tonight's gig had been an early one, a 5-to-9er. So, Tristan had made a date for later. Might as well get something out of the evening. Which means he did everything in his strategic power to make sure no overtime happened. *Give them just enough to love you, but not enough to want to keep going all night long. Exhaust them.* And that's exactly what Tristan and the band did.

Even with his guitar, amp, pedal board, P.A. system with the monstrous speakers and monitors, mics, cables, stands, and music charts, Tristan is rolling out of there by 9:28. That's got to be some kind of record.

As he hauls his gear, compactly arranged on an industrial-sized dolly, every bit of gear tied down with bungee cords, wheels it through the kitchen corridors of the Beverly Hills Hotel, and pushes his load onto the slowest loading-dock lift platform in history, he sees Cyril Brandt coming up from behind.

"Hey, man! How's it goin'?" Tristan extends his hand for a shake.

"It's been too long," Cyril answers, segueing the handshake into a gruff hug. "Were you working that wedding in the ballroom?"

"Yeah, man. And I am ass-tired. I was here for ceremony AND cocktails AND reception, and just barely escaped havin' to do overtime. I've been at this hole all freakin' day. What about you?"

"The Polo Lounge. They're trying out a duo a couple of nights now. See if it increases any traffic. It's been just solo piano in that room for the longest time."

"Do they actually have a piano in there, or you bringin' your own gear?"

"No, they've got a pretty decent grand."

"So, what, they still make you leave through the loading dock, even though you've got no gear?"

"Are you kidding? And be allowed to mingle with the REAL people? D'you just get off the bus, son, or what?"

Tristan laughs. "Forgive me. What was I thinkin'?"

Cyril joins him in a kind of indignant harrumph.

"So, who was with you tonight in the Polo?" asks Tristan.

"Seth Robb?"

Tristan shakes his head. "Naw, man. Don't know him."

"Great bass player."

"You know, it continues to amaze me how many cats there are in this town that I don't know. New one's gittin' off the bus everyday. And they're hungrier than I am, which I guess I should be worried about."

"Yeah, you and me both. Not straight off the bus, though. Seth's been around. I'm surprised you guys haven't gigged together."

"Is he doin' THESE?" Tristan asks, referring to casuals as though they are a naughty word.

"He does everything. Anything that'll pay the rent."

"Straight-ahead guy mainly?"

"GREAT straight-ahead guy. But he's a funky thumper, too. Covers it all. You know, just like us. I'll tell you, he certainly makes the job pleasant."

"Well, I wish I'd had your gig, tonight, I don't mind sayin'. Man, just to get a chance to blow. I need a gig like that again. To remind me I'm human. Nobody houndin' you with idiot requests, no fuckin' protocol, no office coordinators hangin' around spyin' on you like you need a babysitter."

They both cough a consumptive laugh at the ridiculousness Tristan is describing.

And suddenly Tristan's smile drops. "You doin' Hayes DeWitt's benefit tomorrow?"

"Yeah. You, too, huh? Oh, in fact, Seth Robb, the bass player I was just telling you about, he's the one putting this thing on. Talk about your small world. Man, I don't know how he managed to pull it together, but I have this feeling it's going to be huge. Anyway, it's really a shame about Hayes. I heard he wasn't taking the new heart so well."

"Yeah, well, even if it does start to take, and he gets to add fifteen more years to his life, this medical debt is clearly gonna outlive him."

"It's a sin."

"Tell me about it."

Both linger for about a second too long on the plight of being a struggling musician. Every injustice that their friend Hayes DeWitt is currently undergoing, each man knows could easily happen to him. Keeping head above water is just one of the many talents needed to survive their business.

"Anyway, man, I'll see you there then."

"Good to see you."

Tristan can't wait to get into his ten-year old Ford Explorer and quietly turn on some Charlie Christian for his ride back over the hill to Encino, and forget it all. Casuals. Insane brides. Dying friends. Running into other musicians only makes it worse. It invariably reminds him that they are all just little ants scurrying across the anthill, stepping over each other for the crumbs. All to be ultimately squashed someday by some big, oblivious foot.

Cyril Brandt is a perfectly nice guy. Good piano player. Brother Nick is even better. And this Seth Robb guy! Jesus, there are more and more players in this town Tristan has never heard of. It used to be such a small world. No more. What does it matter, though? This is the era in Tristan's life known as burn-out. He is fifty-two years old, a handsome old guitar picker still, who is presently sporting the youngish bleached hair/black roots, bed-head look, a "soul patch" under his bottom lip, and with no hints of a future any more promising than this single moment.

The reward for a thing well done is to have done it.

It is the mantra, from some nameless Eastern-thought philosopher he can't even credit, that Tristan tries to remind himself of whenever he feels at his lowest.

But then there is tonight's date, which has promise written all over it. The night could look up, after all.

A luscious guitar sighs beautifully over his front & rear Bose speakers, as Tristan travels over Benedict Canyon, eventually spilling out into the San Fernando Valley, on this starry black night, and tries to allow this sublime music to remind him why he even bothers being a musician.

NICK

"But hon', you don't understand! I'm the one who sleeps on the couch. I don't get the guest bedroom, because I'm not a couple. You know, I just find it ironical that I am made to sacrifice because I'm single. Being divorced has made me a second-class citizen. I mean, hon', you know I'm not complaining about you, or the accommodations. I'm just making an ironical point that the married couple gets the guest room, and me, the ex-wife, what do I get? I get the couch. I mean, I'm just saying, don't you kinda see the beauty in that ugliness? Yeah. Yeah. Uh huh. No, I know. I'm just saying—"

For Christ's sake, what is that all about? Nick wonders, as he sits in the Goldwater terminal of the Sky Harbor Airport. Can she not carry on her phone conversation, only feet away from where waiting passengers sit quietly with their Styrofoam of coffee and their Phoenix Times without the decibels? Everyone at this gate, before the night is out, will know, in some great detail, that this poor, dowdy, late-fifty-ish mom, in a sweat suit and three purses stuffed like tote bags, is feeling the degradations of being the ex-wife of the newly re-married father of her children. And, from what Nick can piece together, that she's been forced to spend some family event with her adult children, AND the ex and his new bride.

In spite of his annoyance, Nick feels for her. The new bride is probably twenty-five, firm and fit, and without the perpetual kvetching that she, too, will eventually develop in time, as all wives do. And this woman here is no catch. Nasally-voiced and unsophisticated (Nick's greatest pet peeve is when people unnecessarily add that extra syllable to the word *ironic*), she is the fingernails on a chalkboard, complaining bitterly to her child on the other end of the line about the sore accommodations, while at the same time thanking him or her for their hospitality, and thereby creating the very *ironical* situation she has just charged them with heaping on her.

Nick's head is spinning now. Does he always get this involved with strangers' ridiculous soap operas? His own is probably just as sordid. He, too, left a wife, the once beautiful Dorothy Favor, for a younger version, who wound up leaving him for someone who wasn't tortured, embittered, and alcoholic.

Nick is fifty years old, but looks older. He has neither taken great care of himself, nor is he in touch with anything remotely of the new century when it comes to fashion. He wears the same rubber wedge-heel loafers that he's worn since the eighties. He's had them resoled and repaired more times than he can count. And his hair still comes down over his ears, in a haircut that hovers around the same era.

Apathy often dictates Nick's choices in life. Except when it comes to music.

"I'm just saying! No. No. No, you don't understand. He was awful to me! No, okay, maybe not outwardly—no, he never really—it was not like there was something he actually said. It was just—it was in his swagger. It was like he was getting a kick outta being able to parade that trophy wife on his arm, in front of the couch-sleeping loser. No, no, I'm not imagining it. And we're all supposed to be civil to each other? Who was civil? That's what I'd like to know. No, please tell me, because civil does not run in this family!"

The necks, en masse, have begun to crane; the brows to wrinkle their disapproval and annoyance; there are even a few giggles at this poor couch-sleeping loser's expense. Moments such as these always confirm for Nick that he is definitely better off being alone. He has no children from either marriage, therefore no reason to have to face his exes again, and therefore no ties that will ever bind him to the kind of drama that this poor woman is loudly lamenting.

Please, just shut up, lady! he tries to scream, but it only comes out in his thoughts.

He forces himself to think about music. But thinking about music is not the same as hearing it. And frankly, hearing it is not the same as making it. When his fingers touch the keys of a piano, and a warm vibration of that wooden chamber resonates, he knows that he is waking up the beast from its sleep, and making it yawn, and stretch its arms, and open its eyes, and start to speak. And when it speaks, it speaks for Nick. It has no tales of its own to tell, only his. And sometimes the tales are sad, sometimes lovely. Like the song he once wrote for Dorothy, called *She Stayed behind in a Dream.*

Someone should write a song for the weeping phone lady, Nick ponders sadly. Something tragic and wanting and poignant, and which would capture the spirit that had once undoubtedly lived in this woman, but which would foremost sing of her losses, and her desperation to hold onto some measure of dignity.

"Yeah? Well, screw your bastard father and his chippy whore!"

Or not.

Nick chuckles disgustedly at his easy penchant for assigning the romantic to the most banal of scenes. The truth is, this woman isn't deserving of a beautiful song composed in her honor. This woman is crass, loud, disrespectful of all the people sitting around her, who are beginning to fidget in their discomfort, and probably a nightmare for her kids and her ex-husband. Yet here Nick sits, garment bag flung over his slouching lap in the hard airport chairs, about to board his late-night flight home, and trying desperately to find the poetry in this stranger's plight.

He feels ridiculous for the inclination, like it makes him a woman or something. *Fuckin' girl.* His chaotic emotions are nowhere if not found at the ends of his fingers. It is only there, when they are allowed to make music, that the chaos seems to stop. Others know this about him, but even Nick knows it, too. And it is just that very unquantifiable phenomenon that makes him restless.

Elite Entertainment had sent Nick Brandt on a casual in Scottsdale, some corporate party for some bigwig cigarette company. And rather than take his room at the Chaparral Suites after the gig, he'd offered it up to Gary, so both he and whoever he was supposed to be bunking with could have their own rooms (like adults!), and Nick was catching a red-eye out this very night. Fucking Elite was as cheap and penny-pinching as it got in the casual-contracting business. They wouldn't even spring for each musician to have his own room. The chick singer, of course, got her own. When you have the talent to blow the boss, you can pretty much write your own ticket. And the only reason Nick even got his own room was because the band was odd-numbered and he had seniority.

His fingers are tired, and the carpel tunnel in his forearm is acting up again. He hates these flyaway dates, these one-nighters that take a toll on the body and a whole twenty-four hours out of one's day just for one four-hour gig. It doesn't pay nearly enough to merit the hassle. They usually fly you in first thing in the morning, as was the example of this morning, for a gig that isn't until later that night. Phoenix is only an hour plane ride. So, that means he gets in mid-morning, only to check into his hotel room, and have nothing else to do until gig time, except channel surf or go to the hotel bar for a beer...or two. What a waste of his day. He could be home composing. Or going to a bar for a beer or two.

The three complimentary meals they promise you on these

overnighters are usually a lie. It's more like, you're on your own for lunch, for which they always promise to reimburse you (*Right! Just try recouping that!*), a tray of bandwiches for dinner backstage of the event, where there are usually giant risers and scaffoldings and paint cans all around you, providing potential safety hazards, and then a continental breakfast the following morning, provided by the hotel, which means that the office is taking credit for something they aren't even responsible for providing.

On top of all of that, there are usually unnecessary rehearsals scheduled before the event. These people (the clients) have no clue that for a casual you just show up and play. No rehearsal is ever necessary, because you and your fellow musicians have played the same hundred tunes for a hundred years. It's really more for their benefit than the band's; they need to be able to reassure themselves before the actual event that they have indeed hired capable musicians. Of course, Nick's question is always: Don't you bother to find that out before you hire a guy and fly him all the way out here?

The [usually irrational] anxiety of the client has always been a laughing phenomenon amongst musicians. But Nick no longer laughs at those things. He rarely laughs at anything anymore. He worries about his constantly griping malaise, but not enough to actually do anything about it. What better is there to do, anyway, except gripe? Especially tonight, since Phone Lady has already set the tone.

Nick Brandt is especially sunken these days, at the plight of being a musician in this day and age, because his friend is possibly dying from his body rejecting a new heart, and is just plain broke from all the hospital bills so far. Even with ninety percent of the new heart covered by his insurance, the remaining ten percent is still ten percent of half a million dollars.

The fucking guy has played with the greats, Nick thinks to

himself. Dizzy, McCoy, Max Roach. Hayes is one of the greats himself. And yet there he is, at the age of sixty-four, about to lose everything, maybe even his life, if the anti-rejection drugs don't start working soon.

Nick hasn't actually visited his friend to know these things firsthand, not since the surgery. But news like that travels fast in the community of L.A. musicians.

In any case, this should not be the plight of a musician as great as Hayes DeWitt. This is a travesty, Nick stews, and is just what this country has done to musicians.

Tomorrow is the fundraiser that some young kid protégé and worshipper of Hayes's has organized. These fucking things are usually so sad and pitiful. Nick has been to his fair share. A handful of musicians and friends usually show up, some average music is played, and everyone has a weepy story to tell about whomever is inflicted this time. And a few hundred or maybe even a thousand dollars may actually be made by the end of the event, which usually just barely covers the cost of throwing the damned thing in the first place, with maybe a little left over for a meal-on-wheels. In Nick's mind, it is truly a sadder plight than not having a fundraiser at all.

He couldn't've stayed in Phoenix even if he'd wanted to, because besides the fundraiser, at which he has agreed to perform, he has a morning gig first thing, and there is no way he'd've been able to catch a flight back early enough in the morning to make it. Tomorrow is going to be one long day, after this already long night, and all he wants to do is stew and forget.

He finally boards Flight 1339 to Burbank and does his best to get Phone Lady out of his head. *Please don't be on this flight.* She makes him feel so sad. About her. About himself. About Hayes. About this whole fucked-up world. As if he needs any help getting inside that funk.

They aren't in the air fast enough for Nick, but once they hit twenty-thousand feet, he orders a scotch rocks and reclines back in his seat to breathe and sip the jitters away.

A few of these ought to do just the trick.

CHLOE

She sits in her Volkswagen bug outside of the house she has shared with boyfriend Julian Troupe for the past fourteen years. The sky is black and blanketed with flecks of light. It's a moonless night. Hot, and a little humid. She pulls her long dreadlocks up and away from her neck, piles them high on her head like an absurd hat, and leans back against the headrest of her bucket seat. She stares at the restored, three-story, Echo Park Victorian that Julian bought as a fixer-upper in the late eighties right after he'd gotten off the road with Miles.

Julian is the top session and touring guitarist in town, rapidly moving up in the Hancock, Shorter, Hubbard, Corea circles, and is just inches away from some serious renown.

Chloe is a casual singer.

She can't quite budge from her seat, because she realizes that walking through that front door tonight will bring with it more than just her usual arrival home from a gig. Tonight will bring with it a decision she's been needing to make for some time now. She sinks down in her seat and listens to the rough mixes of the CD Julian is producing for her, and isn't quite ready yet to advance forward. She closes her eyes, as she listens to herself on a little six-eight ballad she wrote that Julian arranged. It's her favorite track of the ones they've recorded so far. Gentle. Sparse. Lots of space. And pensive. As pensive as she feels at this very moment.

The gig tonight went well. All things considered. The band even got a tip from the groom's father. As she shakes her head, she suddenly realizes she's made two decisions tonight. Two things that she is presently done with, as of this night, and forever.

When her old college friend DeVoe phoned her two months ago and asked her to contract a band for a friend's daughter's wedding, Chloe was excited for the opportunity to put together the very best musicians she knew; guys who could cut the hardcore jazz and the edgy rock stuff with equal aplomb. She wanted it to be one that the guys would remember fondly, since it is universally agreed upon that casuals can be a real drag. It isn't actually how she feels herself. She is happy for the work. What she's after is approval; that she might be the one vocalist the Boy's Club doesn't call "chick singer," but actually regards with esteem.

"DeVoe, man, thanks for throwing this my way."

"I wouldn't throw it anywhere else. You know me. I can't put together a wedding band. But listen, only thing is, I don't care who else you get. I trust you to hire good guys. But you gotta have me as the guitar player. I mean, these people are, like, family, man. They would bust a gullet to see me playin' in the wedding band."

There must have been some measurable quantum of silence from Chloe after that request, because DeVoe then chimed in with: "Chloe?"

"Yeah, no, I'm here."

"Oh, okay. I thought we got disconnected."

"No, no. So, um, you wanna actually do the gig, huh?"

"Yeah, girl, it'll be a blast. I can't remember the last time we played together."

So much for wanting to put together the best players.

The problem was that while DeVoe is a decent enough guitar player and singer, who's been fronting his own rock band, in several different forms, since the mid-eighties, the boy simply doesn't read music very well and only knows his own tunes.

This is not a working musician. This is a garage band fronter.

What on earth was she going to do with this dilemma? She would never want to hurt DeVoe's feelings. She thought about just thanking him anyway and passing up the opportunity, claiming no time to contract a band, and offer to pass it on to someone else. But frankly, it was too tasty to pass up. Making leader money, on top of singer money, on top of the contracting cut? It would be a better night of money-making than any Chloe could remember in a long time. No, she would simply have to take DeVoe with the package, and find some way to make this all work. She promptly thanked him for the gig, hung up, and sighed, "oh boy."

She then spent the following week trying to decide who she could possibly call for something like this. While she had initially fantasized about hiring burning players, she now also had to consider the tolerance factor, which she knew wasn't always a trait with the most burning players. She'd have to find guys who were not only capable of doing the job, but who would also be patient with the unwieldy circumstances she'd been dealt — that they'd all be playing with a guitar player who would barely be able to cut the gig. If there is ever a weak link on a gig, it makes everyone have to work just that much harder. And guys usually resent that, not only from the musical standpoint, but also because they just don't get paid enough to, on top of their own job, have to prop up some guy who shouldn't be on the gig in the first place. And that guy, this time around, would be DeVoe, Chloe's crazy, pink-haired friend, who was clueless that he'd just shoved her down an impossible road.

Once she assembled a band (decent players, but not the dream band), she then went about the task of trying to figure out what the Hell to do about DeVoe. It would've been so easy to give Phil a call, or Tim, or Ken, or Tristan. She knows hundreds of guys who are great guitar players, who would've been happy to do the job, and who could cut it.

Of course, the big pink elephant in the room, during all of this, was her own live-in boyfriend, Julian Troupe, the best damned guitar player in this damned town. But Julian had made it clear years ago that he never intended to do a casual ever again, after one fateful day back in the mid nineties when he walked right off a bandstand in the middle of a gig. He just couldn't take the trivialness of it any longer.

Chloe has always respected the heart of that sentiment, if not exactly the tactic. So, she and Julian simply never talk about her work, which is almost exclusively casuals.

Not that it mattered anyway, since she was stuck with DeVoe. Even at this instant, thinking back, she hates that this is how she felt about it. They've been dear friends since college. She had some of the best times in her life singing in his punk band in dives like Madame Wong's and the Troubadour, when they were barely legal.

After a few frustrated days of wracking her brain, she called him back.

"DeVoe, I'm just curious why, if these are family friends, why aren't they hiring your band?"

"Man, they don't want our crazy music for Lisa's wedding. We'd give old gramps a heart attack. She wants typical, tepid wedding shit. She wants *Girl From Ipanema*, man."

Typical and tepid. This is what her friend thinks of her living. Moments such as that one every so often illuminate for Chloe just how her casual life is really viewed by the masses. And with it, the dark dawning that sometimes the masses are right on target. The thing is, Chloe doesn't hate casuals. But that anyone would even place his or her ego on being able to get through *Girl From Ipanema* sinks her even further into the bucket seat of her bug. It makes her, for just one second, resent and envy Julian for having finally had the courage to graduate from it.

"But can you even play *Girl From Ipanema*, DeVoe?" Chloe asked at his pronouncement, hoping he would realize that he just may not be up to this.

"How hard can it be, man? It's just a fuckin' casual."

And therein lay the last nail to go ungently pounding into the coffin.

Now that she was essentially stuck with this situation, she decided that she would actually try to get away with never letting on to the other musicians that a neophyte was on the bandstand.

For the next few days, she went about the tedious job of compiling a list of all the standard calls for a casual: Forties swing stuff, Jobim bossa novas, old retread rock and disco and Motown. Nothing too hip could go on the list, like Coltrane jazz or Sly Stone funk. That had originally been her fantasy, if she'd been allowed to put together the guys of her choosing. But with DeVoe along for the ride, she'd have to gather up all the easy stuff, the *typical* and *tepid* stuff, as he'd put it, for him to shed over the next six weeks.

Most gigs Chloe simply books, scribbles in her calendar, and on the day of the event shows up and sings, goes home, and waits for the paycheck. It's all fairly auto-pilot, after all these years. But this gig for DeVoe was turning out to be much more hassle than she had bargained for, as she spent the next couple of weeks compiling fifty or so charts, which entailed Real Books, internet searches, sheet music stores, a late-night all-nighter at Kinko's, and the arduous task of putting them all in a spiral notebook, hole-punched, numbered, etc., and with polite instructions to shed them in every key.

Goddamn it, DeVoe, you'd better be willing to shed these in every key.

When the book was ready, she called him.

And of all the possible scenarios that Chloe could have entertained, the one she never expected was that he would become temperamental and take all of her efforts the wrong way.

"DeVoe, it's Chloe. Listen, everything's underway. I've ironed out the contract with Mrs. Moore, I've hired the band. I've received the deposit. Everything's pretty much ready."

"Cool, man. I knew you were the girl for the job—"

"DeVoe, at this point, there's only one concern left for me."

"Yeah, sure, what is it?"

"Look," she hesitated, "please don't take this the wrong way. But I'm just a little concerned."

"About what?"

"Look, DeVoe, like you said, you don't do casuals. And I'm just worried that…it might be a rough one for you. So, what I've done is—"

"Wait a minute. Am I hearin' this right? You're tryin' to bump me off my own gig?"

"What!? No, DeVoe, I didn't say that! And, and, and, and also, let's, let's make sure we're clear on the semantics here. If this is YOUR gig, then you should be the one booking it, and doing all the grunt work that I've just spent the last couple of weeks doing. I don't mean to sound ungrateful; I deeply appreciate that you threw this my way, but I have worked my ass off to get this all set up, and now all I'm trying to do is provide the best gig possible for these people. And the biggest part of that is making sure the band is tight. And I do have some legitimate concerns here, DeVoe, which I should be able to express without you getting insulted. Now, please just listen to me, okay? You're a great guitar player." (*Very good* is actually more accurate.) "But just because you're a great player doesn't mean you can do this kind of gig. Frankly, it doesn't even take a great player to do this gig. But it does take one who knows really specifically what this kind of gig requires. It requires knowing cover tunes, not originals. And a large body of them! And knowing them in every key. And understanding the basic forms. I mean, it may be the nerdiest music out there, and in many cases it is. But it does require a certain know-how. DeVoe, when have you ever played a standard in your life? Do you even know what a standard is?"

"Man, you're talkin' to me like I'm, like, a dumb shit. I do know how to read music…I mean, you know, I'm not great at sight-reading, but can't you get me the music ahead o' time? Don't you people have books?"

You people?

Oooohhhh! Chloe was about to see red. That he would just leisurely toss off the question as though this kind of thing was simply how casuals went, instead of understanding that it is each musician's responsibility to come in prepared. And that even though — ironically! — she did have a book for him, that it was a huge goddamned hassle for her to prepare this book just for his trifling ass!

Instead, she calmly uttered, "Well, actually, I do have sort of a book for you, but—"

"So, what's the problem?"

Okay, this attitude WILL NOT DO!

But she still needed the job, so she held her tongue and proceeded forward. This was the ass-kissing, spirit-chipping part of her job.

"Just let me get it out first, DeVoe," she said with a calm that was on its way to exploding. "There may not be any problem. But as far as reading a music book is concerned, that's usually allowable for, like, the horn section, cuz that usually means a lot of big band stuff, and there are actual horn parts. But otherwise, generally, no. Guys just have to know tunes. The reason is, you have to be able to maintain a certain flow. You know, you're trying to keep them on the dance floor, you'd better be able to segue right into that next tune, from the last. And there's no chance of being able to make that transition fast and easy, if every guy in the band is flipping pages in his Real Book, trying to find the next tune. That's not to say that some music doesn't have to be read. But you want to have as many of them under your belt as possible, so the gig flows smoothly. Now, if you would just calm down, I want tell you what I've done. And then you'll know that it was never my intention to try to bump you off this gig. Man, I've been working my ass off, on your behalf, to try and find a way to make this gig work. For all of us, DeVoe."

Silence.

"DeVoe?"

"I'm listening."

But DeVoe had already been cold-cocked. And he was still reeling, and too busy trying to check if his jaw had been busted, to be able to truly hear that his old friend had not just betrayed him. He felt utterly betrayed. And humiliated, that her insinuations, while trying their damnedest to prove no insult, were that she was having to bend over backward for the novice, the one who couldn't cut it. And for a goddamned casual, for God's sake! Not something really important. But a *New York, New York – Tie a Yellow Ribbon –You Light up My Life*, shit gig that he apparently wasn't good enough to play. Could it get any more humiliating than that? And as soon as her own head put it in those terms, she realized exactly why he was so hurt.

"Okay," Chloe continued, while DeVoe stewed. "I've actually created sort of a book for you, of songs that will most likely be called that evening. But it's not going to be good enough just to have it on the gig. You're gonna need to familiarize yourself with these tunes. You can have the book there with you. But, you know, try to be off of it as much as possible. If you do that, everything'll be fine. And believe me, that's all I was trying to squeeze in there, before you started freaking out. I swear to God, DeVoe, I so respect your talents. After all these years, you gotta know that. But what I need to know is, after I've bothered to put all this together for you, are you gonna be willing to learn these tunes? Or have I just insulted you so much that you're about ready to tell me to fuck off?"

"No, no," he offered up wearily, and without the usual pep in his spirit. "Sure, gimme the tunes. I appreciate you goin' through all this trouble."

"Look, it wasn't that much trouble," she lied. It was a big lie, too. She'd already stated, in the moment of heat, that she'd been working her ass off, all in the name of DeVoe's limitations as a guitar player. And she knew that there'd been a certain resentment in her voice when she'd said it. But she'd also never heard his voice sound that dejected in all the years she'd known him. And now all she wanted to do was take it all back. Her efforts to try and be the best band contractor in the world had hurt her friend. That was never the intention. After all, as DeVoe had so succinctly put it, *"it's just a fuckin' casual."*

She hung up the phone, that day, after signing off, and felt low. But something also suddenly lifted her worries. She wasn't sure if this made any sense or not, but the humiliation she had heard in DeVoe's voice somehow told her that after all of that, there was no way in Hell DeVoe would show up to that gig unprepared. His dignity would never let it happen. He would determine to prove her dead wrong. And dead wrong she could live with.

As her mind presently races to replay the entire drama, and she adjusts her cramped legs in her bug on the uphill slope of her Echo Park address, and she listens to the crickets outside her car window, she wonders how she ever got through this night without being sued by the client.

And as she glances up to a lighted window coming from her home, she is reminded that DeVoe is only the first half of her dilemma tonight.

SETH

As he drives through Studio City, passing The Sportsman's Lodge, where he's done countless casuals for the lineament crowd, and Jerry's Deli, an old diehard musician hang, he thinks about the first gig he ever did when he'd just arrived in this town, so many years ago now. It was at LaVeLee, which he cranes his neck toward, as he passes by, to see if any music is still going on at this hour. It has always been a fond memory, but for the first time ever he wonders if this thought comes to him every time he passes the joint. He's only driven this stretch of Ventura Boulevard about a thousand times. Associations. Maybe that's why he likes this particular drive. Frankly, you can keep the route that travels up past the Hollywood Bowl, or Forest Lawn, and you can keep the 405 to the 101 interchange, which is never NOT congested, no matter the time of day. These are the various routes that would take him home from gigs, to his dumpy, little Studio City bachelor apartment. But coming up from Beverly Hills, over Coldwater, then heading right on the boulevard, is the best. And now he figures he knows why.

He recalls his first-gig memory as freshly as though he is just driving home from it. He'd gotten a call from a buddy who'd needed a last minute sub, and it was a gig with the hottest Brazilian percussionist in town at the time. Seth had only landed here weeks before, with very few contacts in town, and this stroke of sub luck was pretty much the launching pad to every other gig that currently makes Seth Robb one of the busiest bass players in town. He'd gotten in with the *yo cats*, as much as he tended to hate them. And the *yo cats* had approved. He tried explaining to a singer once on the bandstand what a *yo cat* was, after she overheard him bitching about the overrun of them in Los Angeles. He and the handful of other musicians on the gig that particular evening got a kick out of putting it in dictionary terms for her.

> WEBSTERS: yo . cat (yo´kat´) 1. any musician, specifically of the Southern California brand, who has managed to get into the clique of Jazz/Funk Latin/ Fusion music that permeated the scene during the mid eighties and through the nineties. 2. any of a group of players who usually tends to play the type of jazz that is technically proficient but artistically conservative. You might call him the Young Republican of the jazz scene; diehard bop musicians tend sarcastically to refer to the *yo cat*'s music as *happy jazz* or *jazz lite*. 3. the yuppie brand of musician whose only true passion in life is not his music, but the networking of his music…and his image. 4. the Pretty Boy of jazz, who tends to believe he is the hippest guy to ever loiter a NAMM convention, and who has song titles like *"Samba Breezin"* and *"Song for Ashley."*

"Oh you mean Brady Smith," she'd offered up, putting her own digs into some musician she found to fit that description.

"Oooooohhhh!" the huddle of musicians laughed. They had all known this particular smooth jazz saxophonist, who was prettier than most women, and who perpetually had hits on the WAVE.

Seth Robb is the complete antithesis to that phenomenon, with his grungy, surfer look and his aversion to the muzak those guys churn out for their high-paying, T.V. show, pit band gigs. Seth could never be bothered with that wing of the racket. Even if it meant that he didn't get to land those kinds of jobs. It still means it today, he muses, as he steers his cherried-out reconverted Helms bakery truck into his dilapidated carport, unloads his gear into his garage, climbs the wrought-iron and rocked stair steps, circa 1960, and opens the door to a stuffy apartment. He quickly opens the window that sits in close proximity to his studio gear, and laughs as he observes his own harsh judgments in this quiet instant. Perhaps more of Hayes has rubbed off on him than he ever imagined Hayes would.

Like most other musicians in this town, Seth maintains a home studio. His is better than some, not as upgraded as others. But recently, he has had to stop putting money into it, because the medical bills have begun to completely eat up everything.

After putting his amp and bass away, and grilling himself a cheese sandwich, he turns on his studio gear, and listens back to some stuff he'd been writing earlier. He knows it needs tweaking here and there, but otherwise he's pleased with what he hears. He is supposed to be copping a Bernard Herrmann vibe for this straight-to-video movie he lucked upon scoring. His plan is to try to replace as many sequenced tracks with as many real musicians as he can get away with, but he also knows he'll never be able to do the whole thing live, due to the almost-nothing budget he's been given to work with. As he listens back to a track, he shakes his head in frustration. For, while the writing is decent enough, the application of synthesizers is just not the same as real, live, breathing, FEELING musicians, who will give it serious fire. Especially when it comes to the strings, which are most predominant in this particular cue.

He's already sacrificed much of his own salary to be able to bring in a few real players. By the time this project is over he'll have no real money to show for it, but at least it will be one he can be proud of, as well as another valuable credit for the résumé. When he first landed this film, he was so stoked about it that he started turning down work, just so he could give his one-hundred-percent attention to it, and get everything finished by the due date. But once the project got underway, and his expenses began to outgrow the measly budget, he had to start answering the phone again. Which was why he found himself doing the duo thing tonight with Cyril Brandt at the Beverly Hills Hotel. Cyril is great to work with; they always have a blast together. But all he really wants is to be able to stay locked in his apartment until this score is finished. *Christ, did John Williams or Jerry Goldsmith ever have to struggle this much?* Somehow he doubts it. Some guys just live between the raindrops.

Of course, there is the new snag in this whole picture. Hayes's health has taken such a sudden turn for the worse over the last few weeks that Seth is having to face the decision of whether to disassemble everything in his studio (no small feat), reconfigure over at Hayes's house in Granada Hills, and just move on in. The guy needs someone pretty much twenty-four hours now.

Hayes has his own studio there (who doesn't any longer?), but it's an old reel-to-reel dinosaur of a set-up, and Seth already has his midi files and his music writing software, and his Pro Tools, and all the blah, blah, blah crap that still makes his head spin, in this computer age of music-making. Oh, for the days of manuscript paper and calligraphy pen. And pressing a big, plastic "record" button. And seeing the bright red light come on, that warns "recording session in progress." And actually playing some music! With real guys! And real instruments! How simple those days must've been, Seth muses. He is only in his late thirties and therefore has pretty much grown up in the gadgetry age of digital studios.

But he also has a great respect for this digital age. It is all about time and efficiency. He remembers once being called upon to write a cue for a commercial that needed airing THAT NIGHT. He never even left his apartment for that one. He quickly composed it, all sampled and sequenced, called his

singer friend Chloe to come over and lay down a quick vocal
track, and emailed the producers an MP3 file, who in turn
satellite'd it to New York, and it was a done deal. There he was,
sitting in his beat-up old desk chair that he'd bought at the St.
Vincent De Paul, punching notes from a keyboard one minute;
and turning around, flipping on the remote, and seeing his
finished product flashing across the tube the next. He
remembers that moment of watching the Toyota commercial
that he'd provided a cue for, and thinking, *wow, that could never
have even been conceived of in Trane and Dizzy's day.*

Still. He has always yearned to know what it must be like to
be Hayes's age, and to have played with the legendary cats
(Trane and Dizzy being two of them) that Hayes has played
with. For that matter, Hayes is kind of legendary in his own
right. He was only a scruffy young Black kid from Harlem, a
mere teen, when he officially became the youngest bass player
to have ever played with Dizzy Gillespie. He was the
phenomenon of Lennox Avenue.

Hayes DeWitt is only sixty-four years old. Certainly there
are guys his age still schlepping gear in and out of hotel loading
docks, and playing gigs, and making great music, and exuding
eternal energy. Sixty-four isn't old! But it is for Hayes, who is
currently housebound, ever since receiving a new heart,
debilitated by a legion of drugs, and instructed not to lift his
arms above his chest, which means only one thing for Hayes.
No playing. The one thing that just might kill him, if the
currently-rejecting transplant does not.

Seth knows this about Hayes, without Hayes ever having to
utter it. Seth knows everything about Hayes that any one
person can know. Hayes DeWitt has been Seth's mentor ever
since Seth graduated college almost twenty years ago and began
studying under his idol. He'd heard that the great Hayes DeWitt
was teaching classes, and Seth jumped at the chance to study
under the legendary bass player, whose name is routinely

mentioned in any discussions of the bassist greats; Ray Brown, Charlie Haden, Mingus.

In one of Hayes's classes, they analyzed, note for note, Stravinsky's *Rite of Spring*. This blew Seth's mind the moment he read the class description on the bulletin board at the Musician's Institute.

Hayes DeWitt had always been known as a great bass player, but orchestral guy? With the chops to analyze Stravinsky!? This seemed too good to be true for Seth. And too uncanny. Because that was exactly Seth Robb's background. Like all bass players Seth's age, he had gone through the Jaco Pastorius phase, the Larry Graham phase, etc. They all know how to thump and slap like Larry, and attack rapid-fire modal arpeggios like Jaco. But few in the sea of them could notate twelve-tone matrixes, for example, or dissect the scores of Webern, Ligeti, and Schönberg. Or know what the word aleatoric meant. Few were the odd ball that Seth Robb was. But for one exception — he delightedly discovered all those years ago on an MI bulletin board — his hero, Hayes DeWitt.

Hayes's fledgling film-scoring career had been easily dwarfed by his proficiency as a bass player and his reputation, at one time, for being the most gigging player in town. Quickly, Hayes had ascended to the heights of working with the likes of McCoy Tyner and Max Roach, all the bebop guys from the New York, 52nd Street tradition, and had piles of recordings he could call his own. *Hayes DeWitt, live at the Fillmore! Hayes DeWitt from Shelley's Manne-hole! Hayes DeWitt at the Village Vanguard!* He had early record contracts with Verve and Concord. He had been THE jazz cat. But trying to reconcile that with a career as a legitimate composer proved near impossible.

Hayes chalked it up to racism.

"Of COURSE the brothers are respected for jazz. It's our roots, man. But it's almost like, 'you'd better learn your place, junior, and stay there!' Cuz, you know, the minute I dared to step into that other world it was, like, a joke. And this just might blow your mind, but it was a joke from both sides. Brothers saying to me, 'man, why you wanna play that music?'"

Seth remembers this conversation from so many years ago.

"Well, what did take you to the classical world?" Seth had asked that day, only asking, because he wondered if compulsion worked the same way for everyone.

"See, that's what I'm talking about. Why aren't you asking me 'what took you to jazz?'"

"All I meant was…"

"You're not asking me what took me to jazz, because you assume it's where I should be. Where else do old Black guys go? Right? And if I was a young man, you'd ask me what rappers I was influenced by. It's easier on our brains to stick people in little boxes."

It wasn't why Seth asked the question. But rather than rebut, he simply listened.

And then Hayes paused and thought on something long and hard that day. Seth remembers it well.

"Concert music spoke to me. As naggingly as jazz had. They were the two sides of myself. Speaking to different needs, each. And I would've been foolhardy to follow merely the road expected. Need I say more?"

No, indeed, he did not. The answer rang in Seth's head, because it was his own answer. A smile crept upon Seth's face that day, as it does now. And he knew there was a connection between both men. Something that assured him he was in the right place.

But he also knew then, as he knows now, that Hayes's struggles and frustrations would always ring with race. Sometimes the clangs were loud and obvious. At other times still they might be only tinkles in the far back regions. But they would always linger there. A tease. A warning. A jibe. A tickle. A man cannot tuck his Blackness away for the occasion. And should he? In this case, the occasion would always be the impenetrable film-scoring and concert world.

"How many brothers do you know who are scoring films?" Hayes continued that day, years ago. "His name is Quincy Jones. That's how many. These mother-fuckers are going to make that door impossible to push open till the day I die, aren't they?"

Seth didn't know much about those kinds of struggles, and usually just kept reverently quiet when Hayes went on his rants. But he has always admired Hayes for pushing against society's envelope and delving into a world where a Black man was simply considered a foreigner.

This much, however, Seth did know. It took weight, connections, and nepotism if you wanted to score films in Hollywood. And more importantly, it took not confusing the powers that be with what box you were in.

"Well, what is he?" the powers would ask. "A jazzer or a film composer?"

In their minds, Hayes couldn't be both. It simply didn't happen. So, between that and whatever claims of racism Hayes constantly alleged, he just wasn't about to catch a break.

Now, some forty years later, Seth Robb, accomplished bassist, of the legit *and* popular brand, though hardly of Hayes's fame, is facing many of the same hurdles. Not the racial one, of course, but then Seth isn't all together sure just how much of that has, or has not, been generated in Hayes's frustrated mind.

As he sits this quiet middle of the night, exhausted but supplied from tonight's playing with Cyril (he prefers Cyril's brother, Nick, a much edgier piano player, but Cyril is good, too), the strange path he took as a child suddenly bombards his thoughts. And he realizes that in a very different way, he is as much an anomaly as Hayes is.

Seth was not your typical teen. He didn't grow up listening to rock music, and getting in garage bands with buddies who clunked around teaching themselves (with incorrect technique) how to play their guitars, and screaming into microphones, so they could be the next Black Sabbath.

Seth was never a rock-god wannabe. He was made to take up the tuba in junior high school, for the marching band, which meant his fourteen-year-old head swam with more Tchaikovsky and Sousa than KISS and Megadeth. And he never lost his fascination with concert music. As soon as he could, a freshman in high school, to be exact, he started taking classes at the nearby community college in basic theory, harmony, and ultimately orchestration and composition. He was called a nerd by his rock & roll buddies. Hardly the nerd type (picture parted and greased hair, high waters, horn-rimmed glasses, and pocket calculator), Seth was the exact opposite. He was your classic surfer dude. Long hair. Tall, skinny physique. Hang-10 T-shirts. Keds. Even a serpent tattoo peering out from his socks and crawling up his calf. Looks-wise, he was meant for rock & roll. You'd never guess on first glance of the scraggly teen that Seth's idea of the perfect evening wasn't Iron Maiden at the Palace, but box seats at the Hollywood Bowl for a Prokofiev retrospective.

Not much has changed, Seth muses, as he realizes he still looks like that surfer teen. Now picture that in a tuxedo, and you may get an idea of the absurdity that is Seth Robb when he's doing gigs like the one earlier tonight.

He sits this night listening back to his own writing efforts, and thinking about the odd turn his life has taken: Fledgling composer tying to catch a break in the film industry (just like Hayes in his day), bass player of respectable repute (just like Hayes in his day), relentlessly marching to his own drummer (just like Hayes), and now Hayes DeWitt's personal nurse, for all intents.

When Hayes first fell ill, there was no one to care for him. Hayes has family, but one by one they have each scampered away and out of Hayes's life, probably because Hayes is a difficult man to live with. And the only person left, who felt he was worth hanging around for, was his student, protégé, and friend, Seth Robb. In the beginning, Seth was appalled by Hayes's family, and decided to make his objections loud and clear, not only by sticking around but also by dedicating himself to Hayes's well-being.

It is Seth who takes Hayes to his doctor visits. Seth who runs errands for the old man. Seth who takes charge of the money issues and pays Hayes's bills for him, cooks for him when he can. And now the task is just about to break him. But he will never abandon Hayes.

He probably should've gone there instead of home after the gig tonight, but he feels too exhausted to deal with the orneriness of a bedridden man. Not tonight. Tonight he is tired from gigging, and really needing to work in his own studio, to see if he can get another couple of cues written before going to sleep. The project is due in just a few days, and he has another one waiting in the wings; a spec deal with a friend of his, who has an "in" with a cable movie production. They want to snag that gig, and that means timing. They can't waste time getting something written to present to the music supervisor, and that means getting this one done and out of the way.

Life has to go on, in spite of caretaking for the great Hayes DeWitt. But Seth feels the panic starting, wondering how to successfully juggle them both, and realizing that this benefit tomorrow had better work.

TRISTAN

"What's the most memorable gig you've ever done?" she asks earnestly. Tristan recognizes this tactic at once. He's been through it a hundred times; has employed it himself, in fact. It is the tack all first-daters use in proving their undying fascination with your mundane life. It is meant to boost egos, to nurse and prop, to prime the evening for the possibility of something a little more intimate. With that question, Tristan knows he has at least a fifty-fifty chance of sex this evening.

She's pretty enough. Boob job, obviously, but he doesn't mind that. His ex-wife had a boob job through their entire marriage, since the early days of leaky silicone. As long as they don't have the feel of basketballs, he figures he can get it up.

He'd made it home in time to shower, straighten up the place, and get a blender of margaritas started, before his date arrived, a first with this particular woman. She understood when he explained that he'd have to do this after his gig tonight, so eleven o'clock was the appointed time. This first date wouldn't be dinner and a movie, but he promised her a quiet night, frothy drinks, and the beautiful symphony of crickets that always infiltrate his yard this time of year. So far, promise kept.

Her question is flattering; he can't deny that. It intimates that there is anything at all worth chatting about on the subject he long stopped finding interesting.

They sit on his black leather sofa, watching his favorite video, *Jimi Hendrix: Live at Monterey*, and sipping maggies on this hot summer night. To Tristan, the heat is arousing. It only colors an evening already splendorous with incense, candles, the best music in the world, thirst-and-libido-quenching beverages, and the periodic need to wipe the sweat off their brows. Gnats sprinkle the screen door that look out onto his lighted pool. If things go well, maybe there'll even be a little skinny-dipping in the picture.

"The most memorable, huh?" he answers. "Well, let's see. Should I give you the most ludicrous? The most surreal? The most unbelievably banal? Because if all of those fall under the category of most memorable, we might have a hard time choosing."

The date giggles, takes a sip of her margarita, and inches a hair closer, under the guise of a little cough. Tristan notices.

"No, goofball. The one that puts the biggest smile on your face."

For a minute there Tristan gets scared. Is she expecting some romantic tale of stardom briefly got? Fifty-thousand seaters, and early glory days of rock & roll? Does she think he's some kind of old rock legend she just doesn't recognize, or something? Will she be sorely disappointed to hear that his tales largely involve bouquet tosses and the *Hokey Pokey*?

Is there at least a celebrity or two he could throw into the mix? He's certainly done his share of movie premiere after-parties and celebrity birthday bashes. Let's see. Would she find Whoopi Goldberg's engagement party impressive? Stallone's birthday bash? How about the premiere party for The *Prince of Tides*, and how Babs made sure the band was informed that there were to be absolutely no Streisand tunes done that night, or they'd have Hell to pay! Or the Christmas bash thrown by Kurt and Goldie, and how Kurt was really cool, but Goldie kept screaming at the band every time they tried to take a break? And then one strikes him. *Ah, THIS one should get me in her pants.*

"Well, okay. Here's one. I did one of the inaugural parties for when Clinton took office first time."

"Wow! Really? Did you actually get to meet him?"

"Well, not technically, but he did sit in with the band on his saxophone."

"Oh my God, you actually played music with Bill Clinton! That is cool.

"Well, it was more novelty than music. But there ya' go."

"'Course, I think he's a bastard. But he IS kinda sexy."

Yeah, that he's sexy is just what I want to hear from my date. Maybe I should've stuck with the Babs story.

When Tristan doesn't respond to her comment, except to smirk just ever so subtly, his date awkwardly turns her attentions back to the television, where Jimi is taking it out on *Wild Thing.* Tristan plays this video for all of his first dates. He figures that if they can relate to Jimi, then maybe they can relate to him. It goes a long way toward cutting through a lot of the getting-to-know-you crap.

Not that Tristan is a Jimi clone, as are so many. Sure, he can cop every lick Jimi was known for. Jeff Beck, too, for that matter. He can cop all the guitar gods. But Tristan isn't interested in being anyone's clone. He isn't interested in overworking his whammy bar, or bashing his guitar through his amp. Sure, Jimi was known for monster chops and pyrotechnics, too. What draws Tristan to his idol, what steps Jimi out from the rest, if you ever dare to ask Tristan and have a few hours on your hands, is the undeniably sensual connection that Hendrix had to his guitar. That's what Tristan has always identified with most.

Tristan's own playing is all about the sensual connection. It is the only thing that is truly important, when everything else — the burning chops and mind-blowing technique, the wall of distortion, the facility to float over complex harmonic changes — — tends to be merely a lesson in showboating.

And while Jimi was an electrifying showboater from way back, he also made his guitar simply sing. If Tristan can get his dates to be able to see what he's talking about, if he can get them to watch this video that he's worn thin, and respond with a genuine "wow," then maybe they stand a chance of getting somebody like him — a man whose only true ability to express love (his children, the exception) is through his instrument. Maybe it's silly, this "Jimi test" he always gives. It's the only way he knows how to do it.

He starts to explain some furtive thing that Jimi is doing in the video, when his date suddenly turns and asks him to play for her.

"Why are you trying to woo me with the genius of Hendrix," she utters as if she's heard his very thoughts, and startlingly out of character for what he had already concluded was a small brain wrapped inside a hot package, "when I get the feeling there's some genius of your own that you don't seem to be willing to give me a peek at?"

Tristan is stumped. And flattered. That she is insinuating genius on him, when she's never heard him play. Tristan loves making music for anyone who's willing to listen. He isn't one of those "busman's holiday" guys who are so sick of the casual beat that they don't ever pick up their axes outside of the tuxedo.

And he's even more willing when the request is coming from someone who might be willing to give it up, depending on how much he can wow her.

"All right," he gives in easily enough. He grabs the remote, presses pause, reaches over, and picks up his shiny, two-toned Gibson electric, his pride and joy. He has plenty of guitars: A beautiful blond wood, nylon twelve-string; a lap steel; he's even ventured into the ethnic worlds of Indian sitars and Chinese pipas and xin-xins. In fact, it's what Tristan is known for in the small music community that is his. But his plain, simple, old Gibson electric is sort of like B. B. King's Lucille, for Tristan. It has been through the war with him, for the past thirty years, and has only found its rich voice with age. He plugs it into a nearby amp, slides his pedal board to just beneath his feet where he sits, and smiles at his date, who has helped herself to refilling their glasses. She knows she's hooked him with that request. She is just as interested in his pants as he is in hers.

He might've fared better taking out his acoustic six-string and giving her a little folksy something, which women are always suckers for, but something else has compelled him to want to give her what truly states his sound these days. And to her surprise, it isn't Hendrix-esque in the least.

When Tristan plays, he becomes another part of himself. Maybe not on the casual bandstand, where he generally tends to stay as emotionally detached from the music as possible, and simply committed to giving guests a show-stopping party. On the bandstand it's all about the chops, and the showboating, wanting to entice the party guests into conga lines and Electric Slides and dancing with lampshades on their heads. But when it comes to his own music, he truly does transform into a different vessel altogether. And Tristan doesn't even know it. It's simply something others take note of.

"I'll play you somethin' I've been workin' on."

When he begins to play, his date finds the sounds that come from him somewhat otherworldly. She can't exactly put her finger on it, would never be able to articulate it if asked. It takes a musician's language to do so. But she's heard enough Jimi in her day. George Benson, Robert Johnson. You don't have to be a musician to have heard of these guys. And Tristan's guitar sounds like nothing she's ever heard before. She doesn't know if it's good. But she likes it. A lot. Or she just likes him, and can't be bothered with separating the two.

What Tristan has spent the better part of his mature life developing as his sound is something that comes from being uninterested in showing off amazing arpeggios, like all the flamenco monsters, or distorting the shit out of everything, like every rock god to come down the pike since Jeff Beck.

Tristan has collected a lot of older, classic gear over the years, guitars that most cats might consider out-dated, not cutting edge. And his sound combines a vintage sensibility with an ambient quality that is more about vibe than it is about linear progression. Some guys might say it's just an excuse for not being harmonically sophisticated. A valid argument, except that in Tristan's case, they would be dead wrong. The guys who know Tristan well know exactly what he is capable of. Tristan can handle the most sophisticated jazz gigs, and yet all of the modal complexities that define jazz aren't his heart. And as much as he loves Jimi, rock isn't really his heart, either.

Tristan has been interested, for the past few years now, in the kinds of sounds that once upon a time were the responsibility of synthesizers back in the seventies …BUT…giving those sounds an organic origin. The truth is, he hates synthesizers because there is nothing organic about them. And by that deficit, they date themselves. Every musician can identify, by the very synth sound used, what era a certain recording came from. Everyone was using the flange sound in its day, or the Fender Rhodes sound in its day. What Tristan loves is the idea that guitars are capable of so much more than just strummed chords with a pick, that they are capable of creating such out-there sounds all by themselves. And that the result isn't tinny and fake and cheesy, as is the case with synthesizers, but is rich and thick with texture and environment. He is all about pushing the guitar beyond its designated envelope. And only by way of that rocky road is he able to create music that is sensual and tactical. Music that is about touch and feel and taste. Music that exposes the fragile heart.

He plays some blues for his date, but it is blues like she's never heard it before. No Stevie Ray or B. B. here. And those guys are great. But Tristan's weird head is definitely his own. He uses strange, untraditional changes, and guitar loops that manipulate the feedback. He plays a chord, or a figure, and then presses on his pedal board with his foot to release a loop. And once the loop starts, he never knows what note might come out, or where, or when exactly. He just plays over it. And at times, a chord and a looped note might strike together and make a moment of magic. And it is largely chance, which is part of the charge for Tristan. It is alive. The music has a mind and a voice all its own. Time and space cease.

While he noodles his blues, he tries to explain exactly what he's doing.

"You see, something unexpected can happen, and you find yourself reacting in a certain way. You strum a chord, and then a lick you couldn't possibly have predicted in the loop will suddenly hit, and there's nothing like the serendipity of that moment, which can never be replicated again."

Then he stops talking right when that very moment he has just described suddenly happens. He smiles through it, as he continues to play his blues, closes his eyes, disappears behind the sound, and wins his date's affections in a way he isn't even aware.

This is the Tristan that never surfaces on the casual bandstand. The casual bandstand is all about "being" Carlos Santana, or Prince, or anybody else that might be recognizable and identifiable to a pop audience, who only want to hear their favorites. He can tuck it away for a casual. It's easy to do. But if you ask Tristan Baylor to play something of his, this beautiful madness is what you get.

Tristan is a very manual player: The literal tactical feel of the wood and the strings and the frets and the neck; the way he might strike a sound with his right hand and manipulate it with his left. It is akin to lovemaking for Tristan, and probably no small coincidence that the guitar is a quite phallic thing, indeed. Any guitar playing is actually the perfect segue into an evening of a little romance.

Therefore, when he comes to the close of his erotic (yet

strangely full of pathos) blues, he smiles at his date's gracious applause, unstraps his axe, lays it against the sofa's arm, turns off his gear, and leans in to kiss her. It is the perfect moment. He's been a gentleman all evening, setting a mood for her in his modest Encino home with candles and incense, sharing with her his favorite video, and then giving her a glimpse into his most private self. And never once making an advance that states, *"fuck conversation, let's get busy!"*

And now he deserves a kiss. When he leans in, she is ready for him, as her own hand comes up to his neck, slipping its fingers within the short mane of his two-toned, bed-head haircut, and her mouth parts slightly for his.

The spring shoots right through him, that sensation one feels at the first instant of new touching. A new mouth, a new tongue, a completely different feel from the last girl. This one likes to lightly braze her tongue against his, gently, while the last one preferred a fierce sword-fight of spit-swapping and lip-sucking. They are all different, all unique and utterly poetic in their individuality. Tristan likes the excitement of the new. It never matters how much he might actually grow to like a girl, there will be nothing in their sexual future to top the first kiss, the first caress, the first time his fingers find their way up her skirt, along the skin of her thigh, and into the warm cavern, that first moment of intercourse, when he pierces her for the first time, the first instant his tongue inserts itself in her ear. There is nothing on this earth like the first time. And this moment needs to be savored and lingered over and pampered with a spoiled indulgence.

It might've been so, with an eventual advance to Tristan's bedroom, if Graham weren't suddenly bursting through the front door, carrying a bag from McDonald's and a Big Gulp, and scaring the shit out of the couple on the couch, halting any and all sexual heat in its wake.

"Oooohhh, sorry 'bout that. Don't even think twice, I'm

rollin','" Graham blurts, realizing what he's interrupted. He disappears, just as quickly, into his bedroom and closes the door. But it's all over. No way for Tristan and his date to get back to that moment now.

The date is mortified to've been caught with a hand up her skirt, but only to points of chuckling and covering her face with her hands.

"Oh my God, oh my God, oh my God," she squeals, laughing in whispered horror.

"Shit! I'm sorry about that. I had no idea he was gonna be home this early," Tristan grumps, adjusting the uncomfortable package inside his jeans.

"Is that your roommate? I thought you lived alone."

"I do live alone," he offers in a moment of sore humiliation and defeat of his intention to win this girl tonight. He'll never win her now. Not someone her age. "That's my son. He's with me for the weekend. My daughter, too. She's in the other room. She's been asleep for hours. She was asleep before I even relieved the babysitter. She, believe me, she would not've been an interruption."

"Are you serious?" his date throws out. "There's a child asleep in another part of this house this whole time? And you and I were just about to—"

"Look, I'm tellin' you, she would not've awakened. And even if she did, it's no big deal. We're in here, she's in there. I would deal with it. Okay?"

"And how old is this mystery child in the other room?"

"She's five, and she's not a mystery. Her name is Anna," Tristan answers. At this moment, he is ashamed at himself for being ashamed to be a parent.

"And how old's your son?"

"Seventeen. Look, he was supposed to be gone all night with some friends. And my daughter—I'm tellin' you, when her head hits the pillow, she's out till morning. She's not one o' those up-in-the-middle-of-the-night kinda kids—"

"You let your seventeen-year-old son stay out all night?"

"Okay, look, are we still on this date? Or has it all just gotten way too weird for you, suddenly? Cuz we can either get past the apparently mind-blowing reality that I've got two kids and continue to have a nice time…OR…"

He tosses it off way too brazenly, gesturing toward the door, and showing his mettle, which is none too terribly honorable at this moment. He can't help it. His age, symbolized poignantly by the fact of his fatherhood, seems more and more consistently lately to lose him the battle for romance. And he can't even be angry at fatherhood for it. Because he does, indeed, love his children. So, he blames it on gray hair, and the too many bottles of hair dye that go with the predicament; and aching joints; and hard-ons that barely make it to the three o'clock position any longer; and young women whose jaws would drop to know that he has a son old enough to pursue them more successfully.

As the door slams behind her, with no goodbye uttered on the way out, Tristan stares in the direction of the momentary Lancôme-enhanced tailwind, and feels every sensation, which had boldly leapt out at the instant of their kiss, fold right up, and tuck itself back inside. Date over.

Whatever.

CHLOE

She is still sitting in her car. Still unable to budge, to advance forward, to face the second of her two decisions tonight, because she is still processing the first. Still replaying the events that led up to this morning, with her old loveable, nutcase, acid-dropping, stoner, college buddy DeVoe. To this day, no one has ever learned whether DeVoe is his first name or his last, because it's all he's ever gone by. But all of the traits that had always made him so adorable and quirky suddenly just seem repellent, after what he pulled.

About a week before tonight's gig, she confirmed with all the musicians, gave them their call time, had already cut the checks to the guys so that they wouldn't have to wait around after the gig to get paid, and was all prepared to show up and be vocalist and contractor extraordinaire for a night. She'd left a message on DeVoe's machine as well, but DeVoe never bothered to return the call. He was probably just still stewing, Chloe had thought, shaking her head at all the drama that queen could muster. It was probably his dastardly master plan to keep his distance until the gig so that he could show up, quietly injured, and blow them all away with his shedding chops and recently acquired repertoire. Then she'd have to whimper over to him, with her tail between her legs, and utter all of her *sorry*'s, and her *I-didn't-think-you-had-it-in-you*'s, and her *I-was-so-wrong*'s, and her *you-are-the-king*'s, and her *I-am-not-worthy*'s. And she was perfectly happy to bite that bullet, if it meant that the gig would go off without a hitch.

So, when the phone call came in this morning, the one that changed her life as of that moment, Chloe was bopping around the house, getting ready for her first of a double today.

"Hey, girl, it's DeVoe. Listen, I'm not gonna be able to make the gig tonight," was what she thought she'd heard on the other end, but couldn't't've heard right.

Suddenly, the white-hot flush swept in like a night fiend, washing over her face, swiftly and with no mercy. As it revisits, the same wash of cold sweats takes over again.

Was this some kind of weird humor of DeVoe's? Because if so, he certainly wasn't chiming in fast enough to say "just kidding" so that her heart could begin pumping regularly again. It simply was not possible that after every spun-out, indulgent exchange between them on the theme of her grave insult to him, over which he'd played a brilliant role of wounded indignation, that he would now hand over the baton and willingly submit to his failure. AND that he would do it so flippantly and with an almost "fuck you" nonchalance. Of course, the most mind-boggling phenomenon of all was that the failure in question had, until this moment, been one of DeVoe's inability to play the gig well; it had never even remotely occurred to Chloe that it would end up being about his inability to show up!

And as this pogrom exploded in her head — as she tried to grip the logic behind it; as her panic swelled over the unlikely prospect of being able to find another guitar player on the morning of a Saturday night gig, which is THE prime night of employment for any casual musician, but was a task she had no choice but to accomplish so that she would not renege on her contract with the clients, because they could rightfully sue her for failing to provide the agreed upon number of musicians, and WHAT THE HELL was she going to do, because she didn't have time to get on the horn and find a sub; she had to head out the door for her nooner over at the Jonathan Beach Club — as all of that atomic warfare crashed against the sides of her skull, all that dribbled out of her hung mouth was:

"Huh?"

Of course, now that the gig is over, with no lawsuits in the wind, and even a tip in her pocket, she laughs in this traumatized aftermath at how insane it would've looked to any audience had her brain, in that instant, been a living, moving sitcom.

"Look girl, I'm sorry to do this to you. You know, it's just that I been tryin' to get this stuff down, you know, and it's not that they're hard tunes to learn, it's just, you know, it's a shit load, and you know, I been real busy with stuff lately, and I haven't had as much time as I planned on, to dedicate to sheddin' this stuff, and you know, I mean, you made it sound like, all, like...*it's fuckin' Carnegie Hall, man, and you know, the collapse of civilization is sure to occur if this one little guitar player in the scheme of, like, the great gods, man, like, you know, like, can't cut the theme from 'Love Boat'*. I mean, you just got me all wigged, girl. And I don't mean to let'chu down, and all, man. It's just, you got me feelin' all shitty about myself. And what? I'm s'pose to, like, show up and, and, like, be all nervous to, like, be privileged to be in the same room with, like, all your WORTHY musician friends? You know? You know what I mean? I mean, like, it just wasn't soundin' fun anymore. It was just kinda...suckin'."

Oh my God! Did she hear him right? Did he just turn this thing all the way around to suggest that his choosing to bail on her today was HER fault?

And again, all that could dribble from her aghast mouth was, "huh?"

DeVoe knew how utterly cowardly and irresponsible this gesture was. He was not an innocent here. He may not have been from the casual world, but he knew that what he was doing could cause ramifications she might not be able to rectify, and which would reflect badly on her in the eyes of the client and her fellow musicians. This was his way of paying her back for having wounded him far more deeply than she realized. It had to be. No decent person, realizing the gravity of the gesture, which DeVoe perfectly understood, would choose to bail just because *"it wasn't soundin' fun anymore!"* This was punishment. So, what was the point in appealing?

She simply swallowed her pill — all the while wondering just how much of this she would be willing to forgive, or if this spelled the end of their friendship — and spoke resignedly enough.

"Okay," she recalls saying calmly. "Well, um, okay, it means I don't have time to chat with you, since I've only been given about fifteen minutes to take care of this very major problem on my very busy day. But don't you worry about it, any. I mean, it obviously isn't in your scope to realize that it would be your responsibility to provide me with a capable sub, if bailing was what you absolutely had to do. And like you said, you don't know guys from that world anyway. So, I'm hanging up now."

She hung up the phone, and the panic commenced. She realized that she needed to get on the horn RIGHT THAT SECOND. Jesus Christ, any number of great guys would have made this gig a blast to do. But none of these guys was going to be available at this late a notice. Who the Hell was she going to find? After about ten phone calls, all with the same, *"sorry, I'm already working,"* and the clock running out before she would have to get out of there and to her noon hit on time, she found herself standing at Julian's studio door.

She'd never played the last-resort card with Julian before, yet still she was nervous even to knock on the door.

This is because in lamenting her little drama to him over the weeks leading up to today, Julian rarely had anything patient or understanding to offer. He usually just rolled his eyes and said things like, *"you should be doing better than that crap,"* et al. But never once did he offer: *"I feel for you,"* or *"it's going to be okay, you're going to give those clients a great gig,"* or anything along those morale-boosting lines.

All he ever seems to do any longer is belittle what she does for a living.

But she took a deep breath, knocked, and peeked in.

"Julian, I need to talk to you."

He was closed up in there with his ten guitars, as he is everyday, but is generally always happy to see Chloe whenever she peeks her head in for a little hello.

"I would never, ever come to you with this bullshit if it wasn't a dire emergency. Can you believe DeVoe has flaked on me?"

"I know you are not about to ask me what I think you're about to ask me."

"I know, I know," Chloe said, laughing and pantomiming a noose around her neck. She fully believed that as long as her boyfriend was living and breathing and unbooked this evening, there was at least a contingency plan. Yes, Julian had sworn off casuals, but last minute bail-out emergencies certainly didn't count. So, she laughed at the situation, as if to suggest that while inconvenient, a sacrifice, a favor, it hardly counted as a violation of one's religious beliefs.

"I thought I'd woken up this morning, only to discover that my nightmare was just beginning. Can you believe him?"

"Yes, I can," Julian answered, to make his point that most musicians are flakes on top of being sellouts. But Chloe barely caught that this morning, that subtle paradigm that is so crystal clear now. At the moment, though, she was too busy just trying to rescue herself from drowning.

"I've already tried everybody else I know. So, believe me, I saved you for last. Anyway, I owe you one, baby. You know I would never do this, if it—"

"Wait, wait, wait, wait a second. You act like I've said yes."

Then came the dawning.

"Julian," she offered much more cautiously now, heart pounding, "it's Saturday morning. I have to leave, like, five minutes ago, to get to my first gig. And this gig tonight is in less than seven hours. On a Saturday! Where do you think I'm gonna find any available musician worth his salt to fill this gig?"

"Hmm. A Saturday night free. Worth his salt. Wow. I guess I'm just a loser for being free tonight."

"Oh my God, Julian. Is that where you're going with this? You're home on a Saturday night because you don't do these fucking gigs, not because—"

"Bingo! I don't do these fuckin' gigs! Is it at all possible for you to get that! I didn't break my neck to learn this beautiful instrument, to master its nuances and express what's on my soul, just so I could play the fuckin' *Chicken Dance*, and wear a monkey suit, and count in the fuckin' New Year, and be shoved into the kitchen on breaks for some bullshit cold coffee! You get that? Being a musician means something to me!"

It didn't take saying that being a musician doesn't mean anything to Chloe for Julian to express that very sentiment loud and clear. And this was the very first dawning for Chloe that her boyfriend has no regard for her whatsoever as a musician.

He has no regard for me as a musician.

Her ears ring as she shifts her disappointment from her college buddy (who didn't even show his spineless face at his own friends' reception, even as just a non-guitar-playing guest!) to the man she's devoted her entire adult life to.

She has only spent that adult life living for Julian's every wish. She has put ridiculous pains into garnering his awe of her as a singer. But no, not just a singer. It's always had to be more than that. Just a singer isn't good enough. In fact, the very word "singer" evokes a great deal of general contempt among the community of musicians. And it isn't enough to dub "singer" a bad word. They have to add insult to injury by misogynistically coining the term, "chick singer."

This is what her boyfriend thinks of her. Apparently enough to not care one bit if she ended up being sued by her client and having everything crash and burn on top of her.

If she'd been keen enough, she'd've noticed the subtle, smug upturn of his mouth as he turned back around to practice. But she is only newly keen, under the present clarity of late-night starlight, twelve hours after the disheartening encounter has passed.

As she sits staring at her own home in the wee, dark hours of hindsight, she wonders if tonight will be the moment to do it, or in the morning, after her fried brain has been given a chance to rejuvenate.

NICK

He takes asylum in the earthless, boundless flight of his inebriation. He does not especially view it as an escape from his burdens, as much as a marvelous journey unto itself, bringing with it memories of younger days, more vital days, days of no cares at all except to make a music sublime. And then there is the music. Oh, this journey is filled to the brim with music. The kind you bathe in, not clunk through. Without the journey, always masterminded by Jack Daniels or Glenlivet, there is only the clunking.

Nick spins out of Lot A of the Burbank Airport in his beat-up Porsche, under the merciful influence and feeling reckless, and he heads home, which is only five minutes away. God has exactly that amount of time to decide if he is going to involve Nick in a drunk-driving catastrophe, or let him make it safely to his front door, because Nick has decided in this instant that he is taking no responsibility for it himself. And he is going to challenge God to the highest speed his roadster will push it, for the entire twenty-something blocks to his bungalow in Toluca Lake.

Four minutes and thirty-two seconds later, he pulls into his driveway, stumbles in the front door of his bungalow and does the ritual. Flips on the light, checks his phone machine, fast-forwarding through the social messages and only bothering to jot down the ones that are work related, takes off his jacket, and loosens his tie even further from what had already been loosened earlier in the evening on the plane when the drinking began. He had walked out of his Scottsdale gig, grabbed a cab straight to the airport, and hadn't even bothered to change out of his tuxedo.

He pours himself a drink, sinks into his recliner, and puts on his favorite cut from any recording to come down through the ages, Miles Davis's *Flamenco Sketches*.

He collapses onto his sofa and stares at a photograph on the wall facing him. It is of him and his two brothers, Cyril and Emil, in their first band together as young men. Mutton chops aside, and the fact that Nick is playing the bass in the photo, things have pretty much gone unchanged from that day of thirty-plus years ago. Emil is still a drummer, Cyril still a piano player, but Nick switched over to the piano, too, just a few years after that photo was taken. Older brother Cyril has always been bugged by that, because he was always the piano player in the family. Even their father had played a little trombone. And the point had been for them all to choose different instruments so that they could form a band together. But Nick fouled all that up when he suddenly announced to the guys one day that he'd had an epiphany and was now planning to take up the keys.

Cyril has always accused Nick of trying to one-up him.

"Everything I try to do in this life, it seems you're right there to jump on it, too. Snatch it from me, be better than me at it, steal my thunder, something. I don't know what it is with you, man."

But Nick could give a shit about Cyril's thunder. Cyril is a very respectable piano player, and generally tends to get good gigs. He plays casuals to pay the bills, as they all do, Nick included. He's always cutting a new CD, and getting some little distribution deal somewhere, and selling a handful at gigs. Cyril used to be a personal favorite of the late Chuck Niles from KLON, and genuinely gets the respect and fellowship of his colleagues. He is friendly, he is outgoing, he does the showmanship thing on gigs, tends to jump up and down from his seat during solos and stand to demand an applause when it's over and it's time for the next guy's solo.

How on earth can Cyril possibly think that little brother Nick has any hope of stealing that kind of thunder? Nick is cranky and self-loathing on a good day. Hates gigging, especially casuals, and only just wants to bow his head toward the keys, close his eyes, not have to give a shit about his audience, and play.

He and Emil, the middle brother, get along well, probably because Nick has never threatened to touch the drums. But two piano players in the house? That has meant war for the Brandt brothers.

As he stares at the photo that has begun to fade and yellow from age, he breathes in the Miles and falls intoxicated by Bill Evans's piano, as he recalls a night some while ago at a bar, where he'd finished his last set of the night and was just sitting down for a drink. He got chatty with a lonely lady, who complimented his playing, bought him his drink, and was shortly thereafter getting Nick's life story, which included the woeful rift between he and Cyril, a rift that is by now as aged and yellowed as this photo. But it does still make for good bar sympathy. Especially from lonely ladies.

"Oh my God, you two are the Fabulous Baker Boys!" she chirped, and continued chirping. "Remember that movie? Doesn't that, isn't that, I mean, when you saw that movie, did you just, like, die, and go, *'my God, that's, like, my life up on that screen?'* You saw that movie, right?"

It was at that instant that Nick knew he would not be taking this dip-shit with tits home with him. That goddamned movie had always bugged him. Two pianos! There's never two pianos! In what fucking made-up world are there ever two pianos?

"Look, I don't mean to piss on your favorite movie, but that flick was complete bullshit. There's never two fuckin' pianos. What's the point o' that?" he slobbered in her general direction, to which she responded with a blank look and a slightly dropped jaw. "You would never put two pianos on the same gig. I mean, unless it's, like, a whole rhythm section, and then you might wanna augment the piano with a synthesizer, to do all the string shit and the fake, fuckin' horn stabs and shit. But two grand pianos? Two acoustic, grand pianos? And nothin' else? That's ONLY in the concert world. You know, classical music and shit, where there actually is repertoire written for piano duos. Or maybe, like, back in the days o' boogie-woogie, and cats like Fats Waller, when it was all about showboating dueling pianos. But you know, this shit about, like, playin' Ramada Inns with two grand pianos, and doin', like, fuckin', *Melancholy Baby*? That was the most ridiculous thing I've ever fuckin' seen on a screen."

It might've been short on coherence, but it was ripe with gusto. When he realized that he'd ranted on in a language that was as unintelligible for its inebriation as for its content, he looked her way and caught the dumbfounded stare.

"Sorry. I didn't mean to touch a sore spot," she finally got out, with just a touch of sarcasm. "Y'ever think about seein' a shrink for that one, Joe? Cuz, it's just a fuckin' movie."

And she promptly turned on her heels and sashayed down to the opposite end of the bar.

He remembers that night, of the many like it, clearly now, as he stares longer upon the three youthful Brandt brothers, and suddenly recalls that he had tried to spit back at her that his name was Nick, not Joe, but hadn't managed it before she'd gotten herself out of earshot.

Tonight his head swims with thoughts of scenes that often end badly, and he ponders how, at the close of each, he always winds up alone.

The band he and his two brothers had formed they'd named Pie in the Sky. He stares longer at the three of them, playing some lounge outside of Wichita when he is barely nineteen.

Emil, the drummer, is tall and lanky, but Nick and Cyril have always been short, squatty types. Dark features all three, though Emil has wisps of the dirty blond through his generally brunette, thinning hair.

Dear God in Heaven! Bill Evans's piano playing is just about the tenderest thing Nick has ever heard. It is so sparse. See, that's what guys don't get. You don't have to fill a song with a bunch of shit. Just let it talk to you. It may speak gently, or it may even argue with you a bit. But just leave it alone and let it speak. It isn't supposed to be about showboating, flashing what kind of chops you have. In Bill Evans's case on this beautiful composition, his piano is like raindrops. Or flower petals falling. Or women weeping. Nick can't make up his mind which. But he begins to weep from the sheer radiance of it, until he finds himself stumbling up, heading for the bathroom, and kneeling on his knees, with his head hanging over the toilet, waiting for something to happen.

Flamenco Sketches is the last cut on the *Kind of Blue* album, so when it's done, Nick is suddenly left alone in silence. And the silence is maddening. He wants to play his grand piano right now, but it's two-something in the morning, and he has neighbors with whom he shares a wall. Instead, he waits to pray. Just kneels, hands pressed together, as if in a holding pattern, wondering if vomiting is in his future, and waiting to be cleared for take-off.

When no retching comes, he slowly bows his head.

"Dear God, forgive my sins, which are bountiful and great. And let me find my way to your glory. I'm lost. So lost…"

But Nick Brandt hasn't lost his grace, as he self-deprecatingly claims every night before his toilet, or knelt at his bedside, begging God to redeem him. He just can't seem to realize that it's all in his hands, a set of hands that are easily as magical as Bill Evans's, a set of hands that have always been much more gifted than older brother Cyril's, which is where the real similarities between them and THAT movie lie, and which is the true source of Cyril's discomfort. And Nick hates having to receive the compliments that often come to him from cats who know both brothers, and are constantly whispering their asides that he is the more talented of the two. He can never take those compliments as flatteries. He doesn't want to be better than Cyril. Or worse. Or anything that has to do with measuring them against each other. For Nick, it has never been about one-upmanship. That isn't what playing is supposed to be about.

He weeps and coughs and weeps and coughs so profusely this night, as are many like it, that he can barely get his prayer out. And he wonders if God is able to decipher the drunken mumblings of his coughing fit, enough to hear him and answer.

"Please, Heavenly Father, help me to find the grace that I seem to have lost. I wish only to do your will, Lord, which I know is the way to the kingdom of Heaven. Fuck! Oh, fuck me, goddamn it!"

And the retching suddenly begins, lurching him into a series of convulsions that cramp his ribs.

Where there had been flight, magnificent flight, earlier, there is now only the leaden weight of his self-abuse, and his pinings for God to take away his ache. Please, just take it away!

It is the last thing he remembers.

TRISTAN

Minutes after Tristan's date storms out of the door, Graham reappears, jaw full of burger and amends in his eyes.

"Yo, man, sorry. I fucked up, didn't I?"

"Nah, don't worry about it."

Tristan feels completely defeated, but he knows it isn't any untimely entrance on the part of his son that is the culprit.

"I didn't mean to mess witcha' action," says Graham.

The culprit may, however, be what is about to come next, because he knows that Graham's entrance carried with it some news.

"You didn't," says Tristan. "It's alright. Listen, as long as the date's over, what's the news?"

He doesn't mean for the question to come out like someone waiting for a diagnosis of cancer. He tried for a more energetic segue, but is not a good actor.

"Yo, Dawg, we threw down this track today for d'execs. An' this bad boy was kickin!"

Graham is that anomaly of White kids who do their best to be "gangsta" and much too-conscientiously speaks in the vernacular, even though he grew up in white-bread Canyon Country, just north of the San Fernando Valley by a couple of freeways.

Tristan worried early on that his kid's Santa Clarita Valley upbringing might just breed itself a good, old-fashioned, stripped-Camaro-on-cinder-blocks variety red-neck. Well, at least the kid's gone another way.

Tristan had helped Graham set up a little makeshift studio in his bedroom: Four-track recorder and sampler, is all. It's nothing like the fully equipped digital production studio that Tristan has converted his garage into and does his business from, but is all any kid really needs to lay down his rap tracks and sampled drum loops.

Graham takes one long, sustained swallow of his Coke, belches an even longer, magnanimous tone, flips on his gear to show his dad what he and the boys have been working on, and smiles like he's just had his first sex.

"We got the deal, Pops!"

And there it is.

Graham even delays the sentence as one does a punch line to a savory joke, or a final cadence in a play of the theatre. Timing is everything. Just the proper amount of hesitance in the voice, maybe even a diversionary tactic of making it seem as though the coming news is going to be disappointing, just to create tension and anticipation in the recipient. The recipient, in this case, sees the whole game his giddy son is gleefully playing right now, with this amazing news that every musician should have the fortune to experience some day.

We got the deal.

Within an instant of those words, Tristan throws his arms around his kid and does his best to hold tears at bay. He clings to Graham with a shaky desperation he can't quite decipher, and can't let go. Even when Graham makes the first move to pull away, Tristan won't budge from his embrace. And Graham simply allows his father's sentimental indulgence. How touching and tear-inspiring the idea of not wanting to let go must feel to Graham, as Tristan rewinds *we got the deal* a hundred times in his head. He is a good father. What he himself can't manage to achieve, he only wishes on his deserving offspring, who, early on in his young life, showed an aptitude for music and genius. And now the father is nobly handing the baton to the son, to scale the heights that he has failed. It is a Hallmark moment marred only the glaring, red, blinking sign of bullshit blaring in Tristan's ears like an emergency siren.

He isn't happy for Graham. He knows he should be. Of course he should be. And while his lingering, almost suffocating hug might fool the novice (he prays it will fool his son), he knows it is a gesture that is coming this close to giving away the unstable nature of his own heart.

He can't let go because he is afraid to fall. Afraid to pull away and stare his son in the eyes. Afraid to give away that he resents how cruel life is to hand its pearls to the ones who don't know what it is to have those pearls.

And his mind goes to that place it always goes when it comes to contemplations of his son's stab at the music business. Are the days of feeling music at its deepest core simply gone for good? Is it all, now, just a lesson in the soulless, corporatized mentality that defines youth any longer? Where the criteria for good music isn't about what touches you on a higher plane, and compels you to express, but is instead about what marks the current trend and what thrusts the profit margins off the charts. That seems, these days, to be the definition of good music.

Which, in Tristan's mind, is the reason that most of today's young recording stars are not musicians. They don't have to be. Society doesn't require it of them. It isn't really about making music. It is about assembling the package with three crucial factors: The current urban zeitgeist, gloss, and eternal youth. It has been fine-tuned to a scientific formula. There is nothing remotely organic about it.

In his own son's case, there has never been *the moment*, at least not one that Tristan has ever observed, where music first struck the boy, as it had him. That moment that lays all the Tarots on the table, where the finger points to the card that says, "This moment was always meant to be yours. It was foretold eons ago that music would touch you in the deepest place...RIGHT...NOW..."

Tristan has never seen that moment in his son. Does he always sound this old-fashioned and contemptuous of Graham's pursuits? Is he now officially the very parent who   — as his parents did to him — claims, "I don't get this noise you young people are calling music today"?

He can't stand the idea of sounding like his own father. Does he really hate rap that much? Would he make the claim, as many of his fellow geezer musicians do, that rap can't possibly call itself music? And that the only thing these young kids amount to any longer are cunning opportunists, whose real talents are being able to successfully identify what currently reigns as the king of youth consumerism, and swooping right in like chicken hawks to claim their part in it?

Tristan hates the way he sounds when he thinks on his only son, the rapper. Especially when he has to concede that a little bit of that chicken hawk instinct might've done his own career some good. And the self-disgust sears in him, almost more than the jealousy, when he realizes that he doesn't hate rap, at all. He hates that his son is going to be huge, when he has never managed it. He hates that all of his romantic illusions about great art victoring over mediocrity is bullshit.

"I knew you could do it, man," he warbles into Graham's right ear, voice breaking. He'd better be brilliant at showing his son how happy he is for him. Even if it is just about to kill him. What he knows he does not want to do, as sure as anything, is to discourage Graham from pursuing something that truly excites him, and which doesn't fall into the pharmaceutical, mood-altering, slacker category. At least the kid is involved.

But what he wouldn't give to have his own child feel compelled to pick up an actual instrument — that isn't all about faders and waveforms and meters...and stardom — but is only about the sensual feel of the axe in your hand's grip, or at the grasp of your fingers; and from it the ability to create a sound that is organic and connected to your very being; and the obligation to do it, not because of dreams of stardom, but because your soul demands it.

Or is even THAT fantasy bullshit? If the kid had actually ever shown an aptitude and passion similar to his dad's, and still managed the record deal, would Tristan really be less conflicted?

Or is this just about his own failures?

SETH

When the sun hits Seth's face, he spills out of bed and drives over to Hayes's, where he has his own key so that he doesn't have to wake Hayes. It was a painful rising this morning, but he needs to be there when Hayes wakes up. Today is the big day. Who else but Seth should be helping Hayes out of his bed and into the passenger seat of Hayes's own Lincoln Continental (he refuses to ride in Seth's truck), pack Hayes's wheelchair into the trunk, and personally escort Hayes to the benefit in his honor? This benefit is Seth's baby.

He tiptoes around Hayes's kitchen and finds the coffee maker that will do him good right now. After he makes himself a pot, he moves quietly across Hayes's living room and creeps into Hayes' bedroom, where he takes a seat in a nearby rocking chair and watches Hayes sleep.

Seth feels at such painful odds with his role as caregiver, because his better judgment tells him to give Hayes the best, most nutritious diet he can think of, to ply the old man with pounds and pounds of freshly juiced vegetables, and to detoxify his distressed body with Bentonite concoctions, and to get him on mega-doses of vitamins, colloidal minerals, super foods, enzymes, electrolytes, and herbs.

He spent intense months, during the year that Hayes waited on a list for a heart, reading up on all of the alternative and homeopathic options out there, and especially liked the ones that came from the theory of restoring the body's ability to successfully combat degenerative disorders and general system malaise. He even tried to get Hayes to check out this clinic in Mexico known for its radical detoxification program and its reputation for curing the incurable. Lots of wheat grass, Chinese acupuncture, and enemas. And Hayes would not hear of it.

"Are you outta your fuckin' mind? Nobody's stickin' a douche up my ass."

Not only would Hayes not hear of it with the old heart, but his doctors won't hear of it now that he's got the new one.

Seth constantly found himself butting heads with Hayes's doctors. And after every hair-pulling encounter, he swore to himself that this was the last time he was getting involved with anything deeper than just giving Hayes his baths and serving Hayes his pills. But even back then, he knew he couldn't just sit back and watch the only man who has ever been a father to him deteriorate before his eyes.

The problem, according to the doctors, with Seth's bright ideas about eating organic foods and restoring the immune system, is that they don't want Hayes's system strong. They are trying to encourage the opposite. Otherwise, that mighty immune system Seth is so bent on giving his mentor is going to recognize that new heart as a malicious foreign tissue and start frantically producing antibodies to reject and destroy it. The trick is to keep Hayes's system as weak as possible, which goes against the grain of everything Seth's instincts tell him. So, instead of wheat grass and psyllium shakes, Seth gets the honors of plying Hayes, instead, with a ridiculous daily menu of immuno-suppressants, and anti-rejection drugs, and aspirin for blood-thinning, and Captopril for keeping his blood pressure lowered, and anti-platelet drugs, and beta blocking agents. And it all just makes Seth's head spin to see that many pills ingested by one meek old man every single day. Is Hayes going to have to do this for the rest of his life? And how long will that life be if he's even lucky enough for this current rejection to make a miraculous turnaround? The five-year success rate alone is only about sixty-five percent.

Hayes's insurance is covering ninety percent of his costs, but the price tag on a heart these days is about half a million dollars, not to mention a solid year before the transplant of multiple hospital stays, and the hundreds of tests, and the surgeries, and finally being fitted for a defibrillator, and all the prescription medication, and that angioplasty procedure that didn't work. Therefore, even with health insurance, Hayes is still personally responsible for medical bills in excess of a few hundred grand.

This morning, Seth's head splits wide open from being overwhelmed, and the silence erupts in great gathering billows all around him, trying hard to soothe his temples and quiet his brain. He stares at the sleeping Hayes and thinks back on all that has transpired in both their lives to lead them to this moment, this place — where he would be the one to care for Hayes, and to guide him, and lead him, and instruct him, and oversee him; when for the past twenty years or so Hayes has done that, in spades, for Seth.

It has been well over a year now since he first took the responsibility of caretaking for Hayes. Most days go well enough, preparing Hayes's meals, serving up his party of pills, and driving him to his routine doctor visits. In between, Seth runs home between duties to get as much work done on his film project as he can, tries to grab a nap here and there, gig, and run right back to the Granada Hills house that Hayes had called home for the past thirty years. It has, by now, become an auto-pilot ritual for Seth, but every so often he hits a snag in his will and falls exhausted, body and mind screaming for stillness and silence. This morning is one of those moments, because if they don't raise enough money today to make a dent in Hayes's debt, Seth is all out of ideas.

He looks around the fifties-era ranch-style home, which

evokes memories of his own childhood in a similarly styled house. Each motionless interior glances his way as if to ask him, "what now?" The granite rock fireplace mantle, which hasn't blazed a fire in years, stares at him like a mouth hung open in dumbfoundedness. The dark wood-paneled walls tower above him as if to dare him to let down his guard for one second. The high shag carpet and linoleum entry hall floor both lay before him like two seductresses teasing him and beckoning him to ditch Hayes in favor of a good, long, ten-year nap. And the oversized oaken front door, with the amber-colored beveled glass center, screams, "walk out of here, right now! I dare you to free yourself!"

For all the silence in this house at this moment, Seth's head is filled with sound, but not music. Music might've soothed him. But begging for silence only seems to make the voices begin again, telling him that he is barely up to this task.

Hayes is about to lose this house he's lived in forever, because he isn't gigging and no new income is happening. Sure, he has a little pension plan through the Local 47, but that is piddling at best. L.A.'s Musician's Union is weak, which basically means that being a musician is about never retiring. You can't really afford it. Seth personally knows old cats who blew their horns as their last breaths on earth. Just played right up until the minute of croaking. There is none of this luxury of one's autumn years spent out on the golf course, or taking senior citizen cruises. You play your music and collect your check until the minute you keel over. And if you're lucky, you do it right there on stage in the middle of some burning tune, so that everyone watching can see you go down in a blaze of glory. Not bedridden in some third-rate convalescent hospital.

That's what seems to be pissing Hayes off so much these days, and making him ornery and unbearable. He needs to be playing his upright, not stuck here like some useless invalid. And Seth only stares at the sleeping giant who has changed his life, and feels utterly helpless.

Which is why the benefit today. After everything that Hayes has meant to him, it is the very least he can do.

He makes a few adjustments on Hayes's I.V., then sits back to stare. As he thinks about his life with Hayes, the many roads they've traveled, the battles they've fought, the life that father and son, teacher and student, mentor and protégé, have lived together, all run through his mind like a Super 8 vacation reel, only stopping here and there on the highlights, the ones that today define Seth as a bass player, a composer, and a man.

Summer, 1986. They'd been at this particular film cue for the past eight hours. And suddenly Seth found himself stuck in Room 206 of the Hi-Lo Motor Lodge, down the hill from the city dump, on San Fernando Road, just outside of Sylmar, and wondering how he'd gotten in this predicament. Hayes was working on the score for *Death Mask Massacre VI*, and Seth was his orchestrator, straight out of college, newly acquainted with the great Hayes DeWitt, and suddenly under his wing. He was honored to have the job. Only, Hayes had gotten sick of Seth's presence at his house, called him a distraction, and said he could never work with Seth just hanging around, waiting for something to do. But he did need him close by, because time and deadlines were of the essence.

The next thing Seth knew, he was promptly sequestered in the foulest tenement motor lodge in the dankest armpit of town, complements of Hayes, and ten minutes from Hayes's house in Granada Hills, just waiting for the knock on 206, with reams of score paper for him to work on.

It was Seth's first film, and he was happy to accept the $100 a day Hayes had offered to pay him. He'd already been gigging as a bass player, but he could officially now call himself a paid professional in the film-composing world. He brought over his drafting table, pencils, pencil sharpener, and desk lamp, and made 206 his home for the next two weeks.

His job was to take Hayes's film cues, usually sketched out on three total staves, and fill in the rest, the rest being about sixty other instruments. It was exciting and, frankly, it was the best education Seth had ever gotten in the art of composition – and this assessment was coming from a young kid who'd just graduated music school.

It was because he finally began seeing exactly how Hayes saw music. Seth had just spent the past four years in an academic environment, learning all the mechanics. What a fugue is, for example, with a subject, a counter-subject, and an episode. And he was taught the formula for how each section links together and operates against one another, from a harmonic point of view.

But Hayes saw those deconstructions from a dramatic standpoint, not a technical one. He thought of the melody of a fugue, for example, as a character, who has a relationship with other characters, such as the counter-melody. And he saw them as living in an environment; in this case a harmonic environment. According to Hayes, if all you're doing is labeling those themes, then assembling those labels according to the rules, just as a matter of auto-pilot, what are you really learning? Except to be a technician? You aren't truly connecting to the psychology or the drama of the music. Hayes would ask, why have a counter-melody? And his answer would be that you have this character, in the form of the main melody, and as you experience the music you get familiar with this character. In order for you to keep appreciating this character, you need to be able to get a way from it for a bit, so that you look forward to its return. The episode, in a fugue, would serve that function. That way, there's an actual reason for the relationship between characters, other than, *"that's just the way we're supposed to do it."* Breaking things down to their most base elements and understanding their motives in a dramatic way is Hayes's true gift.

Great composers really understand that kind of stuff, but academics often miss the boat in favor of rules and formulas that govern everything they do. Of course, there are also those "composers" out there who come from the school of, "just put a funky groove under it."

For Seth, this period in his growth had been Heaven, because he not only began to apply these principles to music, but to life itself.

Just because Hayes was great, however, didn't mean he was without flaw. The problems, during that two-week stint at the Hi-Lo, began when Seth would periodically point out mistakes that Hayes might've made in the score. Little things, really, obviously made in the haste of having to meet a deadline. Things like, Seth being forced to re-voice the string harmonies, or needing to juxtapose octaves for a particular melody to accommodate the instrument's range, because Hayes had written too low for the flutes or two high for the tubas. Or having to shorten certain long, sustained notes, meant to be played by the clarinet, because there's no place for the poor clarinetist to take a breath.

The first time Seth made the mistake of pointing out one of these little foibles, Hayes just started screaming.

"What the fuck is this? You're gonna waste my time with some petty shit like, *'the clarinetist needs a breath here, man.'* Just fix it, man! I'm on a time line, and if I happen to miss something that ridiculously small, it might be because I'm having to write an amazing amount of music in a bullshit amount of time. You try meeting the demands that they've given me."

Seth just looked puzzled, and wanted to say, "But I'm your orchestrator. For every note you write, I add about sixty more. So, I AM having to meet those same demands, sixty-fold." But he would never dare offer up an actual argument. He was a barely-out-of-his-teens, wide-eyed kid, working under his idol, who was a great composer, even if he was only landing shitty B-movie jobs. It wasn't Hayes's fault he hadn't had the same breaks as John Williams. Not to mention, Seth was also just the slightest bit intimidated by Hayes, and really didn't want to have to be the target of any more screaming episodes. So, he never pointed out Hayes's mistakes again. He just corrected them, and always wondered if Hayes ever even noticed.

The pressure was on, with Seth writing sometimes as much as forty pages of music a day. Other days he might not hear from Hayes at all. He would just hole up at the Hi-Lo, watch TV, order take-out, and listen to the screaming tenants, and the crying babies, and the boulevard traffic that surrounded him. Maybe even a gunshot or two. The first few nights there, Seth couldn't sleep at all, for the noise. He started bringing his boom box to the room. He would turn the radio dial to the farthest left or right corners, where he could hear only the hiss and static of white noise. It was just enough to drown out that other noise beyond his motel window. And it was to that little bit of clever industriousness that he fell asleep for the next two weeks, even sometimes dreaming that he was near the ocean, instead of smack dab in the smoggy congestion of the San Fernando Valley.

When morale really started to break down for Seth was when he sat down one day and figured out just how much of a favor he was doing Hayes, the man who rarely offered a thank you. He happened to know that John Williams's orchestrators (Williams had a team of them!) were making about $65 a page. Do the math. At an average of forty pages a stretch, Seth should've been making about three grand a day. Not the measly hundred he was making, which, a week before, had seemed like such a deal.

Still, it was the very smallest sacrifice he could make for being given such an invaluable education.

Not to mention Hayes's own fragile morale, which probably couldn't take a dissent from Seth, and which always needed boosting, and which perpetually, and to this day, compelled Hayes toward sour-grapes griping:

"Hell, I can plagiarize right along with the best of them!"

That comment, uttered many times over the years, refers to the fact that if you listen to just about any concert repertoire long enough, you're bound to find John Williams's more signature passages lurking and hiding. The *Jaws* theme, that famous bowed bass figure that everyone has hummed at some point in their lives, is quite prominent in Dvorâk's *Ninth Symphony*. Likewise, the Darth Vader theme pretty much reeks from the pores of *Love For Three Oranges* by Prokofiev. Holst and Stravinsky are liberally borrowed from, as well.

Seth hears those influences, too, and appreciates that at least they are an intelligent influence. But he tends to chalk Hayes's charge of actual note-for-note plagiarism to a deep-seated and tragic case of bitterness. Hayes is every bit as good as John Williams, in Seth's mind, but Hayes is a man who has lived his sixty-four years paying his dues in jazz dives and on B-movie jobs, and making only slightly more, and often less, than union scale. And making his little self-produced albums, which here and there land, usually at the middle-to-bottom rung, on a few minor jazz charts. And truly blowing away the small but worshipful audience he has managed to amass after all these years. And lamenting that he has never achieved renown. And today he lies in a bed in his modest Granada Hills digs, unable to pay his medical bills, which are bountiful, and fearing for his right leg, which has stopped circulating blood because of organ rejection, and wondering if they might not have to amputate. John Williams isn't suffering these poor, miserable, painful, humiliating indignities.

Seth's own thoughts suddenly go to, *"would this be Hayes's plight if he wasn't Black?"* It's the first time his mind has gone there without Hayes's prompting. And he realizes, for the first time ever, that it isn't just a "race card." It is a valid wonder. A palpable sore.

Seth's indulgent reminiscing suddenly lands him square back in the present again, caretaking the invalid. The brilliant, misunderstood, under-appreciated, bitter invalid. And he realizes that it isn't the old sentimental friendship, the one of vital men creating vital works of art for a vital world, but this new one, a friendship of genuine need, and humility, and understanding, and benevolence, that will end up showing both of them the mettle of their worth as men.

CHLOE

She wakes up alone. She can hear Julian bopping around his studio just below them, in their three-story house. He's always the first to rise. She doesn't move. She lingers for an indulgent bit on how she got herself in this place of her great quandary. She is forty years old. She's never owned her own home, or even a brand new car. She has no children, no husband (Julian sort of counts, but there's never been any lawful *"I do"*s). Her commitments and responsibilities are few. She basically lives the life of a college student. Is it because she is afraid to grow up? She's been so set up with her creature comforts that she's never really had to.

During her first years with Julian, in the early nineties, Chloe worked as a waitress at Millie's on Sunset in Silver Lake during the day, and was club-hopping in the cabaret Mecca of West Hollywood at night, taking numbers and sitting in at singer showcases, hoping to get discovered, and going to every jazz gig of her genius boyfriend's. It was, in fact, at one of those, the now defunct Le Café on Ventura Boulevard, that she first fell for Julian Troupe.

She had just moved to L.A. from schooling in New York, where she had begun finding her voice and her love for jazz by sitting in at Village dives, and had graduated with honors from Sarah Lawrence. She'd found a little studio apartment in Miracle Mile, where she spent her days waiting tables or playing on a little piano at home, trying to write tunes, club-hopping to sit in at open mic nights and sing, or just to hear great music and to network. And she'd heard much about the legendary Studio City hotspot.

The café served food downstairs and jazz upstairs, and when she walked in she could already hear the music coming from behind the glass doors up the chrome staircase. It was sizzling. Brushes fondling a drum-head like a warm massage. The deep, warm resonance of a double bass, providing the solid foundation upon which the box guitar could twirl and dip and dance and fly. She quietly ascended the stairs. And as the small but jam-packed room slowly came into view, there in the center of it all was a tilted-headed upright player, a closed-eyed drummer, and the man she would end up sleeping with that very night.

Before her was a chiseled face, the color of perfect cocoa, with years and wisdom carved deeply into it, and a natty goatee surrounding a splendid mouth. He wore neatly twined dreads about shoulder length, with faint streaks of gray.

Black jeans, motorcycle boots, a leather biker jacket, and two pierced hoops in one ear seemed so naughty to her. He was unrepentantly sexy. Not conservatively dressed, like his cohorts, but standing out on his own, commanding notice.

He sat on a chair, with one leg crossed over the other, casually stroking the strings of a rare D'Aquisto. But casual was not the sound coming out of it. He was burning a beatific hole into *All the Things You Are*, and making her fall in love.

She stood quietly, as the song came to its electrifying close, taking care not to distract. The applauding audience was blown away, but Julian never spoke to them. He didn't lean a thank you into the microphone. He barely honored a smile. He just sort of nodded in *yo cat* acknowledgment. A little more than Miles, but less than kind. He then began a soft something alone, delicate and luscious.

A gay couple sat at a table next to where Chloe was standing in the SRO space, and when one of them muttered, "Shit, I need a cold shower," his companion volleyed back with, "You betta wipe that seat off when you get up."

Chloe was in the throes of uncontrollable giggles at their flirty, acidic one-liners, before she was once again caught by this man, over whom these two dandies were gleefully lusting.

Julian's head tilted to the side, during one remarkable solo on an original composition. This was one of those titillating music moments when fellow musicians and laymen alike would slide back in their chairs, as if to be too close would mean to catch the burn of this awesome music. And right in the middle of this solo, his eyes trailed Chloe's way and unabashedly latched onto hers.

For one instant, for one iota of a breath, if time had been allowed to slow down, she swore for just a fraction of a millisecond that his playing stopped.

This is a man whose playing chops have the ability for rapid-fire arpeggios, thus such a second in time would only sound like a skip in a record. But she swore it was there. He continued his solo, however, unabated, ravenous, as he stared at Chloe with a weird intensity.

They made crazy love that night.

It was a whirlwind romance that, by the end of one brief month, segued them into a full-fledged, card-carrying, house-sharing couple. Chloe started dreadlocking her hair and gave up meat, inspired by her earthy new boyfriend.

She quit her job at The Egg & The Eye Café in Miracle Mile and started waitressing in Silver Lake, minutes from her new home, while Julian woodshedded his instrument for fifteen hours a day (still does), and she went to see him gig in the evenings.

That was Chloe's existence. She was actually getting very little accomplished toward her own career, but that was alright. She baked bread, made incredible dinners, burned incense, and kept a lovely home for her lovely man. And at the end of a great day, they had incredible sex. Life was perfect.

When they finally agreed to move in together, they both admitted the quickness of it, but loved the intoxication. They shared Julian's three-story Victorian, where one of the bedrooms had been converted into his studio, in which he'd lock himself, practicing for inconceivable stretches.

He was the hardest-working and most dedicated musician Chloe had ever met. He had unalterable integrity. As a composer, he was cutting edge. As a technician, he had a mind-blowing dexterity about his fingers. And as an artist, he was open and giving when he played, always pushing the envelope, and enticing his fellow players to do the same.

While Chloe had not studied music as her major in college, she'd always played a little rudimentary piano, enough to be able to be self-contained as a songwriter. Just pluck out a few chords, scribble out a chart, and let the band bring it alive. So, she enjoyed when Julian would try to teach her all the modal scales. He wanted to expand her ears so she'd write more harmonically sophisticated tunes, instead of the little weightless pop ones she was trying to write. He was basically a jazz snob. But Chloe never minded that. She was beginning to appreciate the new colors and textures she was coming up with from Julian's influence and his little periodic piano lessons. She liked having him in the role of mentor.

And for a time, life was simply stimulating in the home of Julian Troupe and Chloe Baptiste. She watched and supported the birth of a gifted artist. She saw, in the short span of two years, Julian's rise from Le Café dates to being the opening act at the Playboy Jazz Festival, to getting his development deal with Concord, to playing the Village Gate in New York before SRO audiences, to getting written up by Leonard Feather, no less.

He became quite a buzz in L.A. music circles, regularly

landing session dates for films, and gigging his own project around town, in promotion for his record release. In the beginning, before the Concord contract, Chloe had been instrumental in helping to fill the rooms he played. She contacted the papers and got him mentions in Downbeat Magazine and the *Jazz Times*. He even scored *L.A. Weekly*'s "Pick of the Week." She licked envelopes for hundreds of fliers to be mailed. She arranged for live dates on public radio. She took meetings with companies for sponsorships. And in New York, through some old college connections, she even got him interviewed on Clayton Riley's *Talk Radio*. One inspired phone call got a promoter from Amsterdam down to see him at Catalina's, and from that day forward Julian was on the European festival circuit. All because of Chloe.

She got a kick out of her growing role as Mover & Shaker. There was something empowering about it. People called HER to get to Julian Troupe. She felt like a super agent.

But she also started sleeping fitfully at night. Those rarer and rarer occasions at which she'd play the piano, or sit in at a singer showcase were proving more consistently impotent. She began crying inexplicably at night, and Julian would always offer his concerns, being as good a boyfriend as any could be. He even asked her one day why she wasn't singing as much anymore, though she always got the feeling he never really believed she had anything in her. A nice enough voice, sure. But no real drive, no unerring compulsion to make music. And that lack of drive was the surest way to lose Julian Troupe's respect.

The night that finally slapped her in the face, and told her to wake up and smell her life, was the night of the launching party for Julian's first record release. This was a major event, for which she had worked her ass off to get press coverage and to make sure all the right people got invited. It was held at Linda's on Melrose, an atmospheric loft that featured artists on the walls and an oriental-rug-and-sofa ambiance.

The perfect champagne and Beluga evening, Julian's extraordinary music was being played through the best state-of-the-art speakers around. And Chloe did her meet-and-greet best, like the dutiful girlfriend she was.

A handful of her own friends showed up to be there for her, because they knew that everyone else was there for Julian.

The moment that finally slew her was a moment that could've been extracted directly from the Bible, as many of the most famous public slayings are, because this humiliating grace note in her life happened in front of a circle of people that included her friends.

Julian proceeded to introduce them all to a very important Concord executive. The gentleman extended his hand to Chloe with the standard chitchat question: "And what do YOU do, Ms. Baptiste?"

And before Chloe could open her mouth, Julian placed his loving arms around her and answered (for her, of course):

"She loves me. That's what she does."

BAMMM!!!!!!!!!!!!!!!!!!

And though this happened years ago, on a certain level (distant enough, quiet enough, abstract enough to be conveniently ignored) her ears are still ringing from the great slap.

This morning Chloe rolls over in bed, and is more agitated from going down memory lane than if she'd just gotten up, walked straight into Julian's studio, and told him she was leaving him.

She wasn't able to do it the night before. She had walked in and found him playing. Was he ever not playing? And she couldn't possibly break the spell by…breaking the spell.

That has always been Julian's power over Chloe. As she burrows her head even further into the down pillow, she wonders if he doesn't know this about her, and therefore keeps the music coming just to keep her at a hypnotized distance.

With reminders of that record release night, so many years ago now, Chloe knows there was no real malice in Julian's words. His worst crime, really, on that night, was an ignorant dash of chauvinism, topped with a generous helping of narcissism. But she realizes this morning that it's still going on, more than a decade later. The spirit-chipping methods of a man who doesn't really deserve his genius. Because he doesn't know how to accept it with grace.

NICK

When Nick awakens on the floor just beneath his toilet, which has run all night, handle unjiggled, and stumbles up to a somewhat standing position, it is daylight out. He looks at a clock on the wall, and realizes he barely has time to brush his teeth, make a pot of coffee, and change his clothes. He is just about to be late for his eleven o'clock solo job over at the Ritz Carlton Huntington in Pasadena, which is only about a twenty-minute freeway ride from his bungalow near the studios, but he has slept clear through the morning, and now doesn't have twenty minutes.

Skipping the shower, he trades his wrinkled, vomit-strewn, thriftstore tux for one he actually bought new at the Men's Wearhouse. Though bought new, it has grown threadbare and shiny in spots, over the years, and could use a good ironing, but there is no time. He grabs his cummerbund, stuffs his bow tie in the top pocket of his jacket, sprinkles a little water on his hair, finger-combing it through to achieve some semblance of having actually awakened, and gets the Hell out of there.

Fortunately, this is one of those casuals that doesn't require him to bring his Korg O1W keyboard, his amplifier, his keyboard stand, his music stand, his duffel bag full of cords, and his Xanax. Top 40 and swing band casuals Nick hates. But doing solo gigs he tolerates, because there is usually a grand piano in the room, and all he has to bring is himself. Even doing a solo gig, though, has its challenges. Because solo gigs for a private party, as compared to a club or a lounge somewhere, are still about catering to some client he'd rather not encounter. Some asshole who keeps bitching about, *"it's not the right kind of music for this part of the party. Can you play something mellower while we eat dinner? And then maybe we can kick into a dance set, in between courses."*

Those are the kinds of demands that make Nick see red.

A dance set! You hire a fucking solo piano player, and you're expecting a dance set? You need a full band for a dance set, you moron!

He hates that people who know nothing about music are usually the ones handing out the demands about what he should be playing and how he should be playing it. Who walks into an operating room and tells a surgeon, *don't sew it up this way, sew it up that way?* Is he arrogant to compare musicians to doctors? He's probably spent just as many years as any surgeon studying his vocation, only for his head to be constantly swimming with unqualified voices yelling, *play it louder, play it softer, play it faster, play it slower.*

At least in a club or a lounge, the clientele is there to hear you do what you do. They appreciate you. If they give you any attention at all. And when they don't, if they're just there to chat with their buddies or pick up chicks, that's fine with Nick, too. He never minds just being left alone to make his music. He never even minds if no one claps. But he just absolutely hates when clients of private parties, who've sunk boatloads of money into their shindig, and therefore feel they need to butt in everywhere, start telling him how to do his job.

He skids his Porsche into the valet of the Ritz, grabs a ticket, and just barely makes it to the Georgian Room before the party hostess launches into a full-blown barnyard screech of, *"where the Hell is the piano player I ordered!"*

He sits to the piano, and catches his breath for a second, trying to get his bearings, stop sweating, and get his hands to cease their shaking, which he knows is as much from last night's booze binge as it is from the adrenaline rush of racing to get here. If he gets a bad report from this client, he knows he might be done for. He's already skating on thin ice with Elite Entertainment, who are responsible for the bulk of Nick's income. It's because Nick tends to be late to gigs. A lot. And he is none too diplomatic in the rapport department when having to deal with clients on the job. And he's even been known on occasion to show up to a job buzzed.

But he is also a genius on the keys, so Elite has tolerated him so far. Though, not without the periodic pep talks and reprimands to warn that he can't keep jeopardizing their accounts with his unprofessionalism.

He is just about to have the hostess storm his way, when he lays his hands to the keys, and a sound that would soothe the angriest beast blooms forth. He begins in on *Wonder Why*, and immediately transforms from the growling bear he is famous for being to an angel with wings, upon which a music like nothing else sits and is carried from Heaven's door to Heaven's door.

He begins with an opening cadence that takes awhile to establish the melody, but once he does it is a sweet melody that is just the slightest melancholic. On the second go-round, he breaks into the improvisation over the chord changes that is the staple of jazz. It isn't a busy comping. It is delicate, sparse, thoughtful. It weeps, frankly. And though the smattering of guests who have begun to file into the Georgian Room for somebody's sixtieth birthday, or something, never even notice him in a corner, they couldn't deny, if asked, that the room had invited them and a mood had been created. They might credit the smell of the floral arrangement, or the beautifully set tables before them. But the incredible music coming from a little corner and filling the room from wall to wall is easily the best of it, even if they can't quite put their finger on that fact.

Clusters of minor 11th's and flat 13 - sharp 9th's give *Dedicated To You* a smoky flavor. He even has a few guests throughout the afternoon come up to him and smile, or nod their heads that he isn't being ignored. This is turning out to be precisely the kind of casual Nick likes. *Just leave me alone, and I promise to deliver you something beautiful.*

And at just the instant that he is beginning to feel okay about it all, and he allows his head to lower, and his eyes to close, and his fingers to make magic, and his flight to abound, a guest saunters over, somewhere in the middle of his solo on *You'd Be So Nice To Come Home To*, lays his hand on Nick's shoulder, startling him and abruptly snatching him from his musical reverie, and asks:

"Do you think you could bring some more bread over to our table?"

TRISTAN

"More coffee, Daddy?" she offers, trying to carry the hot pot across the linoleum, and just about to splash its boiling contents over the rim.

Tristan jumps up from the kitchen table and grabs the pot from Anna with a gruffness meant for rescuing his five-year-old from a burn incident and a trip to the emergency room, but achieves instead a crude snatch that sends her into a crying fit.

"Shhh, honey, come on, don't cry. Daddy's sorry. Come on, honey, shhh. I just didn't want you to burn yourself."

"I…just…wan…ed…to…give…you…some…cof…fee…like…they…do…in…westa…wa-a-a-a-nts," she sings with the hill-and-dale wave of child weeping. It churns rhythmically, like a car engine turning over. The more Tristan tries to calm her, the more primal and guttural is the call of the wounded.

It is also too rude an awakening for a man who barely slept the night before.

"Baby, listen to me. Daddy's not mad. Honey, listen. That coffee's very, very hot, and if you spilled it, you'd get burned very badly. Daddy just doesn't want his girl to get hurt. You understand that, right, honey?"

"I…just…wan…ed…to…help…"

"I know, honey. You're very helpful. You're just gonna have to wait till you're a little bit bigger to carry pots with hot coffee in it, okay? You didn't do anything wrong. Okay? You're the most thoughtful girl Daddy knows."

He grabs her up in a flying scoop, launching squeals and jubilance, even as the face is still wet with tears, sets her on his knee to bounce her, and stares into the morning sun out on his backyard deck. The shakes are always with him until the first cup of coffee, but he'll have to save that until Anna is not in scalding distance, for she is unusually boisterous this morning. Or perhaps it's only that he has less conviction to be a dad than usual. He can't help running through his mind the collapse of his evening the night before. It happened in gradations, really.

First there was the discovery by his date of Anna in the next room, which resulted in his not getting any sex last night. His brain can't help assigning blame to this little five-year-old with wispy blond hair and a pug nose and a craving to please her father. He loathes his instincts. Especially because he would choose his children any day of the week over some skank. And because that choice has never been a question before, he wonders with great bitterness why he would even be stricken with the instinct for his brain to go there now. And why does it have to be a choice, anyway? He hasn't had a proper date in months. His children are staying with him more frequently than ever before, primarily because his ex has just gotten involved in a new relationship of her own, and is too busy swimming in the drama that comes with that.

And then, of course, there was the second stage of his evening's collapse. The one that truly knocked the wind out of him and left him on his knees.

At this very moment, Graham and his "crew" are sealing the deal on a label contract with some A&R executive they've been wooing for weeks. Someone associated with Dre's label, or Shug's label. Jesus, Tristan can't keep up with the detritus that calls itself the business anymore.

Graham wanted his father to tag along, but Tristan begged off, telling Graham that he is his own man now, and that his father couldn't be more proud, and that he fully expects

Graham to bring home a bottle of Cristal later to celebrate.

Thankfully, despite the "front" of the tattoos, piercings, pumped up arms, and street cred, Graham is still just a naïve kid who has no clue how painful it is for his father to watch his rise to fame, when the old man himself has never managed it.

And yet, goddamn it, he loves his son! Of that he has no doubt. He wants so badly to be happy for Graham. But he wants the kid to have an appreciable music craft even more.

Oh, really, though?

Or is this very train of thought simply Tristan's way of masking his internal conflicts with something noble, instead of something craven and envious and low?

The truth is, it's both. But the nobler conflict is the only thing Tristan's spirit can stomach this morning without a slash to the wrists for all of his self-disgust.

He realizes in this instant that his greatest failure, far above that of his own career, is that while he might be somewhat successful at luring the women he brings home to his bed with Hendrix concert footage, he has never been successful at luring his own son to any instrument worthy of Hendrix.

And yet the kid is on his certain way to making a splash on every radio station, earning some serious bank, and being wooed with label contracts, and money advances, and tour dates, and endorsements, and shots on *Saturday Night Live*, and who knows what else.

Tristan recalls his own faint brush with a record exec once. It was as a teen in the sixties, probably the same age as Graham now, when his band, The Pogs, got a record executive down to their gig at the Whiskey-a-Go-Go. The asshole promptly signed another act on the same bill, and left before The Pogs even got on stage.

Or the time he got a shot at writing a closing credit song for a low-budget movie, and put his entire savings into the demo session (back before the cost-effective days of home digital studios), only to lose the bid to some studio head's cousin. Or the countless auditions to be the guitar player for some name act that was touring profusely and burning out on their current band. Or the flashy, charismatic front man "guitar holder" who needed a real guitarist in the band to make up for his own lack.

Some of those gigs Tristan got. Some he didn't. None has ever segued him out of the doldrums of struggling musician. He would tour for a few months, bank enough to pay off some bills, and come home unemployable, because "out of sight, out of..."

And as he recalls every one of the moments in his life that teased and taunted him, after he had dedicated his entire life to the struggles and craft of honing his art, he will get to watch from the front row the instant and effortless rise of his son's music career from pimply teenager at the start of this school's semester, to the iron-pumped, tattooed, White-kid rapper that is now all the anomalous rage since Eminem, and who is being wooed, this very minute, by some bigwig, thug-loving music company head honcho who is making his own millions slumming in the hoods of Los Angeles to find the newest ghetto-fabulousness among the hungry, lost teens, dope-heads, and gangbangers. And now Tristan's son.

Anna jumps down and disappears into a sea of toys on the living room floor, while cartoons blast from the television, and Tristan finally pours himself a cup of coffee and contemplates the rest of his day. A play date with Anna at Gymboree, then dropped off at her mother's house. And of course, Hayes DeWitt's benefit, which every musician in town is bound to be at. Tristan is scheduled to perform with his original band, a kind of electronic folk blues project he's been nursing for several years, and in various incarnations. A guitar trio augmented with a West African percussionist, an Indian chanter, and a violinist. Except that all of a sudden, in the early-to-mid nineties, Dave Matthews formed a rock band with a violin, and with all the accolades coming at him about how cutting edge that was, and Tristan remembers that moment back then, feeling like he just couldn't catch a break. And he was more determined, because of the expectation to change, not to change.

So, here he still is. Rural renegade lyrics and a cracked, blues-tinged voice. Personnel has changed over the years, but the instrumentation never has.

His band has developed an arrangement, specifically for today, of one of Hayes DeWitt's original compositions, *Gilead*. There is nothing more honoring than to give a man back what he has given you.

It's a worthy thing that's being done in Hayes's honor, Tristan thinks somberly. And the thought can't help sinking him right back into the flotsam of a musician's significance, because Hayes has basically the same story as most, including Tristan.

There is Miles's autobiography. And Mingus's. Charlie Parker even has a movie made about his life. Hayes is equally as great as musicians of their legend, yet no one except fellow musicians know him. The man is, by all definitions, on his death bed, having lived a long life of making great music, and with nothing but debt, failing health, and obscurity to show for it.

Tristan wonders about that phenomenon. Not just where it regards Hayes, but in general. Think of how much brilliant art we may, as a culture, never get to know about, because there simply wasn't the right-time-right-place fortune for a particular artist. Who even knows how many get stepped over, because there are only so many slots for stardom? Imagine if Rembrandt had never been given a shot at an exhibit; if, Ralph, his painting buddy next door did, instead. Imagine that Coltrane never got a job playing his saxophone, because there were just so many others vying for the same gig.

So many, who are perfectly deserving, don't get the shot. And we'll never know what they might've had to offer culture and the history books. We'll never know what we might've missed.

Oh, but we do get Ashlee Simpson, thank God, Tristan thinks bitterly.

And for that acrid thought, he prays that this event today ends up being awesome, that press will cover it, that somehow, with the threat of this jazz great perhaps leaving this earth soon, Hayes will finally be given his due in the world. This one single event has the power to do it. Of course, Hayes is actually supposed to be there in the flesh. He isn't really on his deathbed, but for the purpose of buzz, to get the numbers there and up, that little bit of exaggeration has been circling around.

Is that going to happen to him, Tristan? Is he going to wake up a decade from now (Hayes is only twelve years older than him!) and suddenly be very old, wracked with medical bills, no spouse to care for him, the threat of losing his house, ending up in some county nursing facility, and dying away into obscurity, having left no name for himself in culture? With all those CDs he's self-produced, just like Hayes? Which have barely ever sold enough to get past the first thousand-pressing, just like Hayes? Hard-earned money constantly being socked away toward the next self-produced CD that only fellow musicians'll buy? The running joke for Tristan, a joke that always stings more than any joke should, is that after pressing a thousand CDs, and with a few years of heavily promoting it on his little rock club gigs, he only has "nine-hundred-&-ninety-six left!"

Every musician he knows has boxes of self-produced CDs sitting in their garages. And if, after all that hard work and honing of craft, the deserving Hayes DeWitt hasn't made it by the end of his life, what hope does he, Tristan, have? At least with jazz, Hayes's music, age has never really mattered. The constellations of the jazz world have always traditionally been old geezers and big fat mamas. Nobody gives a shit how old they are or what they look like. But the rock world, or as close to the rock world as Tristan's music can be categorized, is now dominated by kids his son's age. The only geezers left in rock anymore made their stardom long ago, before they were geezers, like the Rolling Stones or Aerosmith. Or Lavery Snow, rock's newest old geezer, who is the most recent inductee into Rock's Hall of Fame.

"Daddy, when are we going to Gymbowee?" Anna asks, having not yet developed the ability to form R's, and which Tristan finds irresistible.

"Soon, honey, just let Daddy go take a shower. You sit here and watch your cartoons, okay? We're going right now."

Tristan carries a sleep-deprived, fifty-two-year-old body through the master bedroom and into his bathroom. The effects of his coffee haven't completely kicked in yet, shaking the kinks and creaks out of his joints and wiping the fuzz off his brain like a window blade on a car. This is what his morning coffee accomplishes on a good day. On a day brewing with troubles, albeit self-indulgent *why-am-I-even-here* troubles, the effect of waking his body up for the day is usually delayed a little.

The shower feels good on his back, though lately it's begun bugging him from years of having hung a twelve-pound guitar from its strap across the left shoulder-blade and collarbone. His posture has slackened more incrementally over the years, compensating for a rapidly tiring body and general emotional malaise. It is a malaise that crept upon him before he even noticed, until one day he looked up and was no longer rock-&-roll youth, with rock-&-roll energy, and rock-&-roll naiveté, thinking the world was at his feet, and that it was only a matter of time before he would command it with his fingers on the strings, and his bold attack, and his absolute, unbridled stroking of the cock that is his instrument.

By the time the lather covers his body, he's grown sufficiently disgusted with his self-wallowing tendencies. He shakes his wet head, like a dog, until the sides of the shower are strewn with pebbles of foam, and turns his attentions back again to the coming day.

The benefit for Hayes will be a good one, he's decided. If for no other reason than the determination for today to symbolize a life worthy of nursing the artistic instinct, and a life's effort whose reward is for its own sake. Again, back to that mantra that always keeps Tristan just this side of a razor blade.

The reward for a thing well done is to have done it.

Hayes has done it. He has created a music, formed a movement in his day, and shaped the work of many who have followed, all within the span of a single lifetime. And he will emerge from this illness, just a rock in the road, to do it some more. And the world will be a lovelier place because of his presence here. And his will be a music that will last beyond his own life, and into the lives of the younger to come after. Like Tristan's son, perhaps? He should insist that Graham go with him today, and learn about this living legend, who is a friend of his father's. Perhaps by mere association alone, Tristan can generate the respect from his kid that he rarely feels even on the best of days.

SETH

When he first decided to organize this benefit for Hayes, he knew he would have to keep this thing secret. Otherwise, it would never have been pulled off without Hayes insisting, even from his sick bed, on taking over the plans and bossing him around, and showing him the right way to put on a benefit, because no one could do a better job of organizing anything than Hayes DeWitt. Of course, all of that would've been accompanied by nary a thank you, or even just the humble dawning that anyone would want to do such a kind thing for him in the first place.

Yeah, Hayes can be a nightmare. And Seth finally decided that if this fundraiser was going to have any chance of being pulled off successfully, he'd have to keep it a secret, until he could personally chauffer Hayes up to the parking lot of the Musician's Union in Hollywood, which has donated its lot for this outdoor-gorgeous-Sunday-summer-festival-vibe benefit, and have everyone yell surprise.

But at the moment Hayes is still sleeping. Seth chuckles with a shaking head at how much of a prick Hayes can actually be. None of that matters. He is giving the only father figure he's ever had the greatest gift he is capable of offering. He glances at the snoring face, whose eyelids rest atop jittery eyes and tell Seth that Hayes is dreaming. *About what?* he wonders. Is it possible that any of Hayes's dreams include Seth in them? He has been an integral part of Hayes's life for the past two decades. Half his own life. And he wonders just how much of the fabric of Hayes's subconscious he might actually be a part of. Will Hayes leave him in the will? Jeez, just asking that question suddenly makes him loathe himself, even though he knows it isn't material coveting that makes him wonder. He just wants to know how significant a force he's been in Hayes's life. Hayes's own son doesn't speak to Hayes anymore.

Do I fill those shoes for Hayes, where his own son can't? As he is doing for me, where my father couldn't?

Seth's father was a man Hell-bent on letting Seth know what a loser he was. That man has been dead for years now, and when Seth first learned of his father's death, from out on the six-month-long cruise he was working at the time, his reaction was a stunned take, followed by a shrug of the shoulders, a fairly anemic "wow," and a continuation of the plate he'd been filling at the buffet table.

He knew the guy had cancer, and it was expected at any minute, but he and his father had stopped speaking years before that. Yet when the moment came, as he sat down in the galley break room for musicians to eat his meal, he stared at his food and felt as if he'd lost something. But what had he lost? His father had been a prick Seth's whole life. He had beaten Seth and his mother many times in drunken rages, who both spent their entire lives under the roof of this man, always tiptoeing around, making sure not to stir the beast. Some existence. Until Seth was old enough to get out of there and never return. He skipped even before he got out of high school, and begged his mother to skip, too. But she was so woven into the fabric of her only familiar that she just bore up. Seth has always felt that she was simply counting her own days, as in, *"what other life is there for me at my age? I'll just bide my time till one of us gets old and dies."* His mother has never actually said those words, but he's always gotten the feeling that this was the sentiment.

The very first thought that came to Seth at the

announcement of his father's death, besides his own confused feelings on an event he always thought he'd celebrate, was that his mother was finally free. Once the cancer had debilitated his father, of course, and he was moved to hospice, he was at least out of the house. But her obligation as wife continued her to be there with him everyday, though the old man, himself, loathed it of her.

Eventually Seth cried for his father. It might've been days after, weeks after, or months after. He can't really remember. But he did. And he hated the man even more when he couldn't control his tears and his grief, for having created such an emotional quagmire in the first place.

"Why am I sad for this bastard who only ever abused and destroyed?" he cried in those weird days.

And he eventually came to realize that his tears were because if there was ever a shot at a miraculous turn-around for Brian Robb to make amends, atone for his sins, and be a father to his son, that chance was now forever gone. And, perhaps most soberly of all, that it was a chance missed not because it was time's fault for running out, but because Brian Robb had no intentions of seeking redemption before he died. And Seth realized that what he was grieving for was the loss of someone who never was.

The man on that deathbed, a stranger to Seth, went out feeling smug and justified for all of his loathings toward his family, a loathing Seth never got.

You made us! You assembled this family by seeking out a bride and giving her a child! Only to…what?...resent us for anchoring you?

But Seth has never known the answer to that one. He grasps at straws. Exhaustedly. And always will.

As he stares at the man sleeping in front of him, he realizes that Hayes is the first person in his life to care about seeing him grow as a man and accomplish something. Hayes is the first person ever to nurture and be proud of Seth, in spite of the orneriness, which harkens all too often on Seth's father, and may even be the reason Hayes's own family is nowhere around any longer.

We all have our demons. The ones in our heads and hearts, as well as the ones in the flesh. Maybe Hayes's son has tales to tell on his father. It's been easy for Seth to dismiss the son and the wife as a disloyal bunch, until he reminds himself what he had to do, once upon a time, for his survival.

Maybe Seth's father, Brian, had taken some other kid under his wing and told him he was worthwhile, in a way he could never tell his own son.

But why? Why all this confusing displacement of loyalty? Why so willing with a prototype and not the real thing?

Seth has been asking these questions to his burdened mind for so long now, and without any answers. And of course he realizes that he asks questions of a phenomenon he may very well have just created in his own head.

Whatever the phenomenon is, he is grateful that someone has come along in his life to love him. His mother's love has always been there, of course, in the only scared way she ever knew how. They shared a common plight, that's for sure. But a man needs his father. And now Seth has his.

And he will, damn it, make this day the greatest Hayes has ever known. It's the very least he can do for the only person responsible for Seth being the man he is today.

For two solid months, Seth's life has swum dizzy in all the details regarding the benefit: The rental of a stage and a tent; the catering; calling around to music stores to ask if they'd be willing to donate the use of a sound system; fliers; contacting all the music magazines, which barely gave him the time of day, even though we're talking about Hayes DeWitt, for Christ's sake!; trying to get Unicef and the Red Cross and the NAACP involved; investigating how to protect the money raised from being taxed, through funneling it into a non-profit company;

setting up that non-profit company; to the most pain-in-the-ass task of all — lining up the talent.

Fucking musicians!

They think they're misunderstood? Treated like the hired help on most gigs? Unappreciated? As much as all of that may be true, they're also just a bunch of whiny, prima donna babies.

Hayes spent most of his musician's life playing with the greats and cutting his own records, but he also played casuals in between road gigs and composer session dates. It's what you have to do when you're a freelancer. So, his circle of comrades ranges from the everyday guy, who is just grateful to be in this town making a living as a musician, to the truly unmanageable egos of the elite few who have claimed a name here.

Bill Fitzmorris insisted on getting paid, complaining about the overhead of his drum cartage. Sure, Bill Fitzmorris is up for the Sting gig, and just got off the road with Sheryl Crow, and made the cover of last month's Modern Drummer. Big fucking deal. This is a fundraiser! For a great musician of more fucking note than Bill Fitzmorris will ever have! Money needs to be coming in, not going out. But Seth also knew that getting Bill Fitzmorris would draw every drummer in town to this thing. They all follow him around like he's the fucking Pied Piper. So, though he can barely afford to pay his own rent this month, Seth is now paying for Bill Fitzmorris's cartage out of his own pocket. Excellent!

As for the bass players, forget it. Most of them in town, of any weight, probably studied under Hayes at some point. And yet, getting them to come and perform with their various ensembles, or even to generate some kind of mini bass clinic as a part of the day's events, was a ridiculous hurdle. It is ironic that Hayes used to try to instill in his students the philosophy that you have to have contempt for the world. It's the only way, according to Hayes, that the world will respect you. If you need a gig or an audience too much, they'll turn their backs on you.

Ironic because now every bass player who ever studied under Hayes is pretty much doing their best to put that philosophy to the test. It isn't that they haven't been willing to participate. But the lot of them have fought and scraped for the prime spot of event closer, or put in their bids to be the one to do a Hayes retrospective, *"because who really knows Hayes DeWitt better than me?"*

Yeah? Well, where are any of you when Hayes can't be left alone for fear of collapse? Where are you to deal with his chronic digestive problems? The constipation caused by medication, or the diarrhea caused by organ rejection? Or trying to force food into him, because the nausea takes away his appetite? Or giving him his lukewarm sitz baths, which Hayes screams and yells about, because a hot shower might just upset his internal thermostat, which needs to stay stable?

Where have any of you fuckers, *who-know-Hayes-better-than-anyone*, been?

Of course, it's easy to get worked up about the ones who've made it difficult. The truth is, most of the musicians Seth approached have not only cooperated, but have expressed feeling honored to have been asked to be a part of this momentous occasion.

Many even came forward on their own, once the news got circulated that this was being planned. Musicians that Seth doesn't even personally know, but who have long history with Hayes, worked on *this* movie session or *that* road gig with him. As well as the ones who up until last year, when the last heart attack took him down, had been doing casuals with him, and always found him a legendary joy to be on a bandstand with. They not only offered their services to perform, they also offered to serve food, circulate fliers, donate equipment, whatever Seth needed.

Balthazar Brava even offered to park cars! Of course, Seth wouldn't hear of it. But Balthazar-freaking-Brava! The legendary drummer, in his own right, who has played with freaking Bird! And is probably old enough to be Hayes's father.

Hey, Bill Fitzmorris! Pay attention! This is how you do your famous life with class, you prick!

Whatever. All the others, the ones who have offered to help in any way they can, are the ones who remind Seth why he loves the community of musicians that are his community, and make him feel as if his hard work might actually pay off.

His cell phone vibrates.

"Hello," he whispers, as he tiptoes back out into Hayes's living room.

"Hey, Seth, it's Chloe. How's Hayes? Is he ready for today?"

"Well, actually, he doesn't know about today. It's meant to be a surprise. Although, I do wonder if everyone in town suddenly yelling surprise out in the parking lot of the union won't just stop his new heart."

They both laugh, even though Seth feels conflicted about making such jokes.

"He's doin' alright though. You know Hayes. He tells me to fuck off about ten times a day. Actually, I'm at his house right now, so I can't talk too loud. But they've got him on tons o' drugs, man. He must take fifty pills a day. I swear to God. It's just such a pollution of his body."

"He's lucky to have you there."

"Who else is gonna do it? He's pissed his whole family off. You know the kinda prick he can be."

"I know he's done a lot for you, Seth, but you've done a lot for him. And he knows it. He appreciates you."

If only she could know the depth of what that comment conjures in Seth.

"I hope you're right. More than anything, though, I just need this thing to come off without a hitch."

"Oh, it will, don't worry about that. Speaking of it, though, the reason I'm even calling is that I've got kind of a personal crisis of my own brewing today—"

"So, you can't make it," Seth interrupts with unintentional disappointment in his voice.

"No, no, no, no, I wouldn't do that to you. And I wouldn't do it to Hayes. But I just wanted to warn you that you may or may not get Julian's cooperation today."

"Goddamn it, Julian's name is gonna draw people. What's the prick ranting about now?"

"Well...nothing. Yet. Aagghhh, you know what? I'm sorry I even called you with this. With everything you must be dealing with today? Please, don't even worry about it. I'll just, I'll just— I'll make sure Julian's there. I didn't mean to throw this at you right now."

"Are you and he not doing well?"

"Oh, you know, I've barely gotten outta bed yet. So, it's hard to say. You kinda have to approach Julian like you do AA. One day at a time?"

They both chuckle that burdened laugh that is the symptom of a heavy life. Chloe and Seth are old friends, and each has followed the trials of the love life of the other for years now. A woman had only just recently walked out of Seth's life, a flight attendant he'd met coming home from a flyaway date about a year ago. If he hadn't been so wrapped up in Hayes's situation, he might've been sadder about it. But Seth is the "oh well" kid. He shrugs his shoulders, doesn't allow warmth to get near enough to melt the iceberg, and for it stays alive and relatively unharmed.

But he also knows that his friend has been struggling to keep her longtime relationship together. He's been there, too, and he doesn't envy her.

"Well, whatever's goin' on, I hope you two are okay. And we're gonna make some great music today, right? For Hayes."

"For Hayes," comes the response on the other end, as if toasting their old friend.

When he hangs up the phone, he hears moaning from the other room. Often Hayes will wake up and not know where he is for a minute. The confusion causes him to moan about and struggle with his covers, as if he's been kidnapped and is trying to break free.

"I'm right here," whispers Seth. He knows that the delirium is only momentary. Hayes will be his ornery self again in minutes.

Can't wait.

Seth moves close to touch Hayes's forehead. Even the briefest of human contact can often snap a person right out of his euphoria. Hayes opens his eyes, a pair of sunken orbs that have become slightly cataract. They roll around, trying to get their bearings and fix on one solid thing. Before they can fix on Seth, Seth has moved to the window to open the blinds.

"It's too goddamned bright," Hayes mutters, each word linked to the next by the lazy gross motor skill of his tongue and teeth. The meds.

"The light'll be good for you. It'll help wake you up, and show you what a beautiful day it is. I was thinking about a drive this afternoon, what do you think?"

"Don't talk to me like I'm a goddamned baby!"

Hayes is as irascible as ever, Seth notes, as he stares from the window. He doesn't respond. He realizes that Hayes might be talking to anyone. It isn't a personal dig. It's a clumsy attempt to regain some sense of self that Hayes must feel he's rapidly losing; a bold assertion of the rascal Hayes is kind of famous for being, and which has accounted for most of what people lovingly tolerate in him, so that they can get close enough to be touched more deeply by what is truly great in him. He's never realized that the doorway is still open for the world's accolades, and for intimacy, without the rude frame. That in the end, it really is all just about his great gift as an artist, and his great capacity to offer love. But the crankiness is all he's ever known, and he now latches onto it, to the rudeness and the impatience, as if they are the very key to his resurrection.

And that's just it. Hayes has every intention of resurrecting. Of parlaying the twenty-five-year-old heart he's been given into eternal youth. Of rising from the dead to pick up his seven-foot concert bass again, an irreplaceable German beauty that was crafted in 1726, lean into it as one bows to royalty, with a tilted head and a magic at his fingertips, and beckon music forth as effortlessly as when he was a young man.

Seth knows that Hayes's curses are meant for God, not him.

"Hey! Seth Robb."

"Yeah. I'm here." Seth sits next to Hayes on the edge of his bed and adjusts the levels on his I.V.

"Seth Robb is one of my students, you know."

Seth looks his way. Looks in his eyes, which still seem to be struggling to latch onto something. Hayes isn't here right now, he realizes. It happens sometimes. But it's not as though Hayes has Alzheimer's. His mind is fine. Sometimes the medication makes him fuzzy. But it doesn't usually take him back that far.

"Hayes," he whispers, as he touches Hayes's forehead again. The touching seems to anchor Hayes. "It's me. Seth."

"I know who you are," says Hayes, looking directly at Seth now. "You hear the one about the blue-blooded, Ivy League White woman who suddenly starts craving ham hocks, collard greens, and chitlins, after receiving the heart of a Black man?"

Hayes starts laughing even before he finishes his joke.

Seth laughs with him, then offers, "Yeah, well, old, crotchety jazz snob that you are, it'll serve you right if you just all of a sudden start breakin' into some country-western pickin', which I know is your personal favorite."

Seth also starts laughing before the end of his sentence.

"My son's coming to take me for a drive today."

And suddenly Hayes is gone again. Where, Seth can't figure. Hayes's son hasn't been on the scene in years. Seth sits and watches Hayes closely to see what might come next. Seth wants to think that because of his invitation to go for a drive, only moments ago, that maybe Hayes's confusion is linked to his associations with Seth as being like a son.

He realizes that his hopes are vulnerable, fragile, feminine. He hates the inclination. Why do our parents fuck us up so?

NICK

He finishes up his set with *Stella by Starlight*, takes a break, and wanders over to the bar of this private affair, wondering if he can score a drink without any hassles from Frau Coordinator. Unfortunately, to his discovery, there is no bar. This is a champagne brunch, and the beverage simply circulates the tables in endless refills. But champagne does not grab Nick anyway. He needs a stiff one. He ventures out into the long corridor of the Ritz Pasadena and glances out to the Japanese Garden, just beyond a huge picture window, that sets gently in the center of the hotel. This time of day, a little past noon, is awash with a fresh sunlight, as the day's smog hasn't had the chance to mar its purity quite yet. Wait until about four o'clock, when the freeways get their worst, even on Sundays, and the sunlight not only begins to reflect a dullness in light, but in the moods and tempers of all who are at its mercy. Right now, there is a peace that Nick can't help but breathe in.

As he passes the garden on his right, he heads directly forward to the hotel's lounge. He recognizes the beautiful blonde behind the piano, doing her regular Sunday job, and nods to her respectfully. She nods back. Even if she can't exactly place him, she knows he's a fellow player. The tux always gives it away.

There was a time when the very unique ensemble, long a staple in high society, spelled highbrow. And it always made even the dowdiest man look dashing. No longer. The casual musician has successfully managed to snatch that bit of magic from the power of the tuxedo and turn it, instead, into a morphed symbol of laboring servant.

One way to easily identify a musician in a tuxedo from a party guest in a tuxedo is to take note the stylishly careworn black Nikes he's sporting instead of dress shoes. Another is to observe the mismatched jacket and pants, usually found in a bin at an Aardvark's thrift store. They will invariably, in rummaging to find that magical garment ensemble, unknowingly match a navy blue jacket with black pants, or vice versa. Nick laughs at the thought, having made that very mistake.

Everyone knows that musicians, like their canine counterparts, are universally colorblind. Of course, only in certain sunlight can you really tell a black-on-blue ensemble, which makes for nervous cocktail hours or afternoon ceremonies out in the sun-drenched gardens of some of Beverly Hills's plushest hotels.

Guitar players and bass players have a special little added garnish to their tuxedo look: The worn-away, frayed, shiny spot right at the place where their axe rests against their torso. Nick calls this "axe erosion."

Then there is the black-jeans-with-tux-jacket look, a particular favorite amongst drummers, since they're rarely seen out from behind their trap set, and so figure they can get away with it. Nick's own drummer brother, Emil, keeps his tuxedo balled up in his trap case. The thing has probably never seen an iron or a dry cleaners, seeing as it has likely never left his car.

The truth is, no one is requiring Armani or Hugo Boss for the job. It actually takes very little money to dress nicely and find a decent, off-the-rack tux in good shape, and Nick knows it. And it takes no money at all to properly match the colors (it simply takes the absence of the dog gene, which is probably asking too much).

The real reason guys are perpetually ragged looking, and therefore easily spotted by their fellow players, is that there is a kind of weird pride for them in looking like crap. When you're tired, burned out, slightly beaten down by a surreal world—where brides are a frightening species of their own; where bratty rich kids, who have tens of thousands of dollars spent on their bar and bat mitzvahs, are given the carte blanche to treat YOU like the child; where your dignity is constantly being chipped away by some barnyard screeching maître-d who practically slaps your hand for taking a dinner roll from a platter full of them, or for approaching the bar for a club soda; where they scream at you to go to the kitchen, and not to fraternize with the guests, but the kitchen hates you because you're in their way—when all of this is your reality, what's your only recourse?

For Nick, it's kind of like flag-burning or armband-wearing. He sports his rag-tag look with proud indignation, and that's really all that's needed to make his silent statement of irreverence loud and clear. It's a code of solidarity amongst musicians. If Nick looks too nice, he might actually be mistaken for someone who gives a shit.

And here, finally, is the light bulb that illuminates the entire paradigm of Nick Brandt's life.

Wow. A tangent that long and bitter requires a drink. He regards the beautiful piano player once more. He doesn't know her name, but has run into her here and there over the years. And suddenly, as he lifts his foot to the tap rail and rests his elbow over the bar to indicate a need for service, he instantly discovers why he doesn't know her name. She probably only does this gig, and that's it. She isn't really equipped for much else. He notices with a weariness that her time is wobbly. She is the classic symptom of the solo pianist who is unaccustomed to playing with others. She has no time to consider but her own unsteady one. But in this woman's case, Nick hears another reason for her waxing and waning tempo. She speeds up where she's feeling unusually confident about the coming passage, and slows down when confidence wanes. There is no actual consideration of the mood or sentiment of the song in designing one's dynamics, only the reflection of a novice who just happens to be good-looking enough to have landed this job. Her chord changes are elementary, but Nick doesn't give a shit about that. Some of the simplest harmonic vocabulary in the world has produced some of the loveliest compositions. But he knows that fear is what leads her to simplify everything, not artistic choice.

He wants to go over and tell her something. He doesn't want to tell her to go take some lessons and get some modal ideas under her belt, all the advice another piano player might offer. He wants to tell her to be bold. Don't give a shit. Don't care that a fellow piano player has just walked in this room and has judged you harshly. Just close your eyes, forget about the asshole, only regard the music, open your soul, and let inspiration in.

That's what he wants to say. And maybe take her home later, for a night. Instead, he orders a scotch rocks.

Nick rarely takes anyone home anymore. Nick Brandt has lost his fire. Much more comforting to indulge in memories of the past anyway. Like the days of being married to the best jazz vocalist this town ever saw, the inimitable Dorothy Favor. And accompanying her, where the experience was like none he's ever been able to match since with any singer in this anemic town. Dorothy knew how to bleed when she sang. She knew how to make you bleed. But it was a good kind of bloodletting. You came away from a Dorothy Favor experience baptized and redeemed.

He thinks and speaks of her, when he does, as if she is past tense. But Dorothy Favor is still a working vocalist in this town. New gigs that open up in new places don't even consider her, as she is of a certain age. But she has held one of the rare club steadies in this city, at the downtown bar The Orchid Club, for nearly twenty years. The only act to hold a gig longer is The

Dresden Room's Marty & Elayne. But Dorothy is no novelty act. She is the real thing. Even if for Nick's heart's sake, he must think of her as no longer here.

Since those days, his only companionship has been the one-night stands he has as a lengthy résumé. Banging waitresses at bars he's hanging out at until closing, when the owners have to ask him to leave. Even a singer or two, though he loathes the lot of them. And he'll tell you he loathes them because most of them are obnoxious divas who take for granted that their instrument, the voice, is something they are simply given at birth, and that no such honing or cultivating of that instrument, such as learning the basics of harmony and theory and how to read music, is needed. So, they believe that it's everyone else's job to know all that academia shit, and to provide them with their microphone and cable, and to bring them a chair, so that they can sit in between songs and fan themselves and just generally be waited on hand and foot.

He'll tell you that's the reason. But the truth is, Nick loathes them because they are not Dorothy.

And now, even the effort to bang chicks that he doesn't have to invest any heart in has pretty much dissipated.

Today, the only thing that gives his heart or body the ache enough to pursue it with any energy is the demon rum. Though, it usually comes in the form of scotch. Maybe Jack Daniels.

He listens to the blonde beauty clunk skittishly through *I've Got the World on a String*, and yearns to plop right down beside her, and take her hands in his own, and lightly rest them on the keyboard, and beckon her gently to just breathe and let the song play itself. But his break is nearly over, and his resolve to engage deadened by the drink. One more set to go of his own shindig in the Georgian Room.

He takes one last swig, nods her way again, and strolls back down the brightly flooded corridor with the view of mini Japan to his (now) left, and wonders how he got himself stuck in L.A.

He knows how he got here. His father was a musician, who moved the family from Indiana in the late fifties when Nick was just a boy. But how did he get so stuck? So wedged into the bear-trap clamps of L.A., and unable to wiggle free? At least in a place like New York, or even Montreal, there are still jazz clubs by the droves. That used to be the case here.

Carmello's, Donté's, Simply Blues, Shelley's Mannehole, Vine Street Bar & Grill, Le Café, Nucleus Nuance. Man, what a town this used to be!

And the only answer Nick can come up with for why he didn't get out sooner is that eventually you just start sprouting roots under the earth. Not so easy to simply pack up and leave, even if that's what all the jazz clubs ended up doing.

And now there are barely any of them left here today. There might be a couple of bar lounges that usually house easy-listening piano players, like the pretty blonde. At least they leave you alone. Nick suddenly envies her. He had a solo steady once at the Peninsula Hotel. But there's no more music there now. Brother Cyril has just started a duo gig at the Beverly Hills Hotel. See how long that lasts. One by one, they all go away.

God, he can even remember as far back as the days of the Mocambo, in the mid to late fifties. He was only a kid at the time, but his dad used to play that room. Those were the days when the big bands of Count Basie and Artie Shaw were the house orchestras. Who has a steady big band gig these days? Is there anybody on this earth who employs that many musicians on a regular basis any longer?

And as he strolls back into the Georgian Room and sits to the piano for one last set, starting in on *So Many Stars*, he realizes bleakly that the answer is:

Yeah. Casual contractors.

TRISTAN

Showering, he lazily slaps some soap to his arm pits and crotch, rinses his two-toned hair of its shampoo, twice, and lingers his way out of the mildewed shower stall, unwilling to face the day with any real charge.

After drying off and slipping on a pair of jeans, briefs either forgotten or purposely avoided in the cruel conspiracy to keep him forever clinging to brash youth, adjusting his equipment to one neat side, haphazardly flinging a tee over his creaking but relatively muscular shoulders, and assaulting his hair with bed-head gel, he grabs his tennis shoes and walks back to the living room. He stares at the only person in his life from whom he feels complete awe and devotion, as Anna watches *Spongebob Squarepants* with a partially dressed Barbie hanging by its mane from her right hand, kind of forgotten, but never completely abandoned. He sits on the sofa and absentmindedly puts on his shoes.

And when was the last time he even thought about Lavery Snow, rock's newest Hall-of-Famer, he suddenly wonders, referring to his earlier musings about old rock geezers. Ohhhh, it is never going to leave him alone, is it?

Lavery Snow was Tristan's best friend in high school. They formed bands and penned loopy rebel-raging songs together in their youth. They were, in fact, the stars of their high school, and it was always Tristan and Lavery, Lavery and Tristan. They may've even lost their virginity together, to a couple of beautiful twelfth-graders, at their sophomore year battle-of-the-bands, but that particular night is still an acid-dropping haze for Tristan.

There is a dream that used to plague Tristan for years, and it lasted as long as it did because for a minute there (several years to be exact), he actually believed in its possibility. Tristan had lost touch with his old rock-band buddy shortly after graduation, but that buddy has remained in Tristan's consciousness over this past thirty-five years, with a merciless bombardment, because Lavery Snow is now a multiple Grammy-winning musician, with an Oscar nomination, platinum records, a couple of famous actress ex-wives on his résumé, and a fairly constant presence in the tabloids.

For years, Tristan followed his old friend's growing fame with a pride usually reserved for parents at a talent show. And he always fantasized about the day when they might run into each other again, after all the years, and hug gruffly, as men with a bond do, and share old war stories, and Tristan would genuinely offer, "if it could only be one of us, man..."

And maybe L. S. would even share this sentimental surge and ask Tristan to come on board and tour with his band. And he'd introduce the unknown Tristan Baylor to an adoring crowd of fifteen-thousand at the Universal Amphitheatre with something along the lines of, *"please welcome an old friend from my youth. We were the Lennon and McCartney of our day. And it's high time we were that again. We've taken different roads to meet here tonight, after many long years, but I have never forgotten my old partner."*

And in this recurring dream, the crowd goes wild because they adore L. S. and would adore anyone he adored. And there would be, in one magical moment, the opportunity Tristan had waited for his whole life.

And the first chord strummed would instantaneously tell the fans that it was simply luck, and not gift, that had taken L. S. where it might've taken T. B. And they would be blown away and wonder where this guitar phenomenon had been hiding all these years.

That particular dream rewound and replayed itself for years, until about ten years ago. When one day Lavery Snow strolled through the outdoor restaurant of the Hotel Bel Air, where Tristan was at the time maintaining a duo gig, playing acoustic chamber music repertoire for the Sunday brunch crowd. On the afternoon in question, Tristan looked up from an especially difficult cadence on a Segovia piece, and saw his old friend for the first time since high school, as famous as ever, and flanked by a couple of other music and movie notables. Tristan dug his haunches into the earth and geared for the moment he had literally dreamed of for years. He knew that while Lavery Snow had been in the public eye for a good two decades now, and was therefore hard to forget, Tristan had not been, and would surely require the temporary jogging of the brain before Snow would remember him. After all, neither man presently looked as he did in high school.

Snow didn't look their way, Tristan's and the other guitarist's, who sat side by side on chairs, playing their classical guitars. Tristan's instinctive response was: How does a fellow musician not even look up to acknowledge live music in a room, if for no other reason than that he is one of them?

But Lavery Snow was definitely not "one of them." He was no longer a musician, the craftsman of music, the moving form, defined by its very word as the adjective essence of the muse, which is to be muse-ic. And to BE music is what Lavery Snow no longer was. What Lavery Snow was, was a rock star.

No matter. It certainly wouldn't be the first time people strolled right past or sat at their brunch tables, never noticing that live music was only four feet away. It's just that Tristan reserved his special contempt for rock stars, pop stars, and Grammy winners, who were once musicians and therefore had no excuse.

And so, on the afternoon in question, Lavery Snow, who

didn't notice them, headed with his entourage toward the exit. Tristan politely begged away for a moment, placed his guitar horizontally on the fold-up chair and made his way toward Lennon's McCartney. Or McCartney's Lennon. Didn't really matter. At that moment they were Joe Celebrity and Joe Who?

As he relives that day, the day that stopped the dreams, Tristan doesn't have the stomach to revisit the actual dialogue that was exchanged. Suffice it to say that Lavery Snow was polite enough, but had no recollection (or maybe a vague one, the claim of which is the obligation of the diplomat) of any friendship with this hotel employee. He certainly acknowledged that there had been bands he'd been in as a youth, but that faces, places, and spaces were but a dim, pot-fogged memory any longer, and to please forgive him.

But what stunned Tristan the most was that there was no natural curiosity, that curiosity anyone would have if a seeming stranger walked up and said that you'd known each other, of, *what band were we in together?* or, *who did we used to hang out with?* Some little nugget that might actually bring it all back. You see, one actually has to be interested in remembering.

Instead, Lavery Snow smiled, as if it would be better not to be rude to the obsessed fan, shook Tristan's hand even as he was inching toward the valet, but as gentlemanly as men at the corporate tables of war do it, and floated away on his magic carpet of celebrity.

Since that day, Tristan and Lavery Snow have been in the same room (he gigging, L. S. famousing) of various hotel lounges, restaurants, and private functions time and time over. And never again since that first time has Tristan tried to approach. Therefore, neither man has spoken to the other. Not because of any deliberate shunning on the part of the rock star. It is simply that Tristan Baylor is invisible to Lavery Snow. There is neither the recollection of the old high school kinship of yore, nor even that of the brief encounter at a swanky hotel in the relative present. And every one of those moments is the stab just to the right side of the heart that says to Tristan that he merits not even a childhood remembrance from the friend Tristan obviously never touched.

"When you touch someone's life, they don't forget you."

"What, Daddy?"

As he realizes he just said that out loud, Tristan is jolted back to the present, to his daughter, to his home in the San Fernando Valley, to his son's awesome news and good fortune, to his music. To his life. This is where he needs to stay. Not over there, in the never-comforting land of what-if's and why-not-me's, but here, where the music he creates is important to him and bears no compromise.

He looks up to Anna, who has spilled the tumbler of orange juice that Tristan had left in her charge when he went to shower.

"I spilled, Daddy, but I'm cleaning it up," says Anna, with *uh-oh!* on her face.

"It's okay, honey, Daddy's got it."

Tristan takes care, with multi-tasking skill, of putting on his other shoe, forgotten in the wake of his self-wallowing, and grabbing a dish towel from the kitchen in one splendid move.

"We don't want ants, right?"

"Wight!" Anna barks, as if part of some exuberant plot.

She is exclusively his. Of course, he shares her with a mother. God saw fit in his mischievous folly to require a woman to produce a creature as lovely as his Anna. But she is his very own (shared with no one) adoring fan club.

The reward for a thing well done...(in this case, his loveliest little angel)...*is to have done it.*

CHLOE

She's gotten as far as the shower, realizing that once she's actually facing Julian this morning she won't really know how to act, since she's pretty much decided to end this once and for all, but has, at least for now, promised Seth (who doesn't even know what she's planning to do) that she won't do it today...for the sake of the benefit. Oh, who is she kidding? It didn't take much convincing, since she's just a big old coward. Instead, she does everything in her power to move through her morning rituals like a snail. To avoid Julian until she absolutely has to face him.

Julian agreed to have his ensemble play at Hayes's benefit today, and Chloe is supposed to sit in on a couple of tunes during their set, with originals from the CD she and Julian have been working on. Her tunes. But Julian's arrangements. His band. His touch. It's really more Julian's record than it is Chloe's. As is everything in their life together, she suddenly realizes.

Once she tells him it's over, how on earth are they going to reconcile this project they've been working on for two years now? For that matter, they've sown every piece of fabric of their lives together for fourteen years. There will be so much more than just a recording project to divide.

But if she tells him right now, she fears he won't agree to play with her at this benefit. Or maybe she won't agree to play with him. She wants him very badly to be the villain here, but maybe it's her, for planning to pull the rug out from under him. And maybe she's the one who will behave with pettiness and refuse to be in a room with him, once it's all out in the open.

And then, as well, if somehow it all went remarkably well, and they still agreed to show up together to play for the benefit, what's the good in bringing all that baggage with them to this thing?

But this is her life. A life that's been virtually hijacked, and which she needs to get back badly. What's more important than dealing with that?

She stands against the wall in the shower and cries. She hurts so badly at the idea of walking away that her stomach cramps and she sinks slowly onto the tile floor of the shower. She has loved this man for so long that she can't even remember when her feelings for him started. But when she reminds herself that this is her second summons in a lifetime, the first being the instant of that stringent blow back ten years ago, that *"she loves me, that's what she does"* moment that gave her stunning clarity, she also realizes that she is pretty damned slow to learn a lesson.

She recalls that night of ten years ago, again, and that the summons had read Chloe her dawning loudly. She remembers it like a loud gong in her ear:

For some, it is enough to feed and nurture the greatness in others, to help plant a seed, and love it, and water it, and talk to it, and prune it carefully, and attend the mulch, and then stand back and watch it grow.

For some. But not for you. Not anymore. Your own music, YOUR voice, YOUR axe, has gathered dust. And so has your spirit.

She remembers walking away from that evening a stunned woman, and though she knew that she still wanted to support this extraordinary man and his music, she signed up the very next day for a singer's workshop she'd read about on the bulletin board at Hollywood Sheet Music. Early nineties this was, and it was time to stop waiting tables.

It was just a workshop. There were hundreds in the city, all touting, "we can groom the star in you!" They usually never did, of course. They just took your money. And they didn't often give singers any real foundation to get work with, like teaching music theory, or how to read or even identify the key of any song, or emotional interpretation and understanding how to connect internally to music. They taught marketing. Which wasn't a bad gift to have, but it was all about making celebrities, not musicians. And Chloe, for all her dreams of record tours and Billboard charts, wanted to be a musician. She wanted the respect of her boyfriend, if no one else.

So, this workshop never really gave Chloe much. Except for an introduction to a fellow singer/workshopper, who had been very complimentary to Chloe the first time Chloe had gotten up to sing in class.

"You have a great voice."

"Thanks, you too."

"My name's Maggie. Maggie Fortune."

"Wow, what a name."

"Yeah," Maggie laughed, "you'd think that with a name like that, I'd actually be somewhere in this life, wouldn't you?"

"Well, with a name like that, I'm sure you will be. I'm Chloe Baptiste."

"What a name for you, too. Are you French?"

"Creole. Which is close enough for Black folk, I guess."

"Sure. Hey, listen, are you gigging much these days? Do you have a song list?"

"A song list?"

"Yeah, a repertoire. Tunes."

"Oh...I...um...I mean, I have a handful under my belt. You know, stuff I always take to open mic nights. Mainly, you know, I'm trying to work on my original project. So, you know, I'm trying to write a lot toward that. Kind of more of a jazz vein."

"Really? Mmmm. Interesting. No, cuz like, jazz just isn't really selling much these days, is it? I mean, like, vocal jazz."

Chloe's eyes grew wide at the sass and pepper coming from this little Versace in high heels, who had determined in one hasty word that all of Chloe's creative efforts were in vain.

"But if you have any standards, you know…that I could use."

"Use for what?"

"My husband Andreas and I have a contracting office, Fortune Music Events. And we're always looking for singers. But the thing is, see, nobody gives a shit about original projects. I mean, no offense."

Maggie Fortune was a feisty New Yorker who took bullshit from no one, and must've been Gypsy Rose Lee in another life. Within minutes of seeing her in action, Chloe knew the woman drank twenty cups of coffee before noon. Maggie was, according to her own claims, merely the talent scout for her husband's business. But Chloe had no doubts that it was only a matter of time before this fireball would be CEO of Fortune Music Events.

"Do you mind if I speak to you bluntly, you know, just between us girls? Cuz, like, I think you and I are past all the Hollywood bullshit."

Past all the Hollywood bullshit? Was this woman for real? They'd barely gotten through one workshop and a meet-and-greet, but of course there was certainly enough history between them to merit being past the Hollywood bullshit. Chloe was already beginning to identify the self-preservation of Maggie Fortune's crass little character. Because, the only thing that *'past the Hollywood bullshit'* meant was that Maggie was giving herself permission to be further obnoxious, and Chloe couldn't wait to hear what more little stabs she had to offer, if for no other reason than the fascination of the not-to-be-believed audacity.

"Sure. Speak freely."

"Well, it's just cuz I think you're worth hearing what I have to say. And really quickly too, cuz I gotta get outta here. How do I say this? Get yourself a REAL repertoire. Okay? It's as simple as that. You do that, and you can actually work in this town. I mean, it's not gonna make you famous. But you're past that, right? I mean, cuz you know, if you're not eighteen and already on the Billboard charts, it's not gonna happen. You know what I'm saying? Not in this day and age. I mean, yeah, sure, in the jazz world, it probably doesn't matter how old you are. But, like…IS there even a jazz world any longer? You know what I'm saying? I mean, that's the point I'm making. Jazz is fine, and all. But let's live in the real world for a minute. It ain't sellin'. Not to any significant market. And what is it, anyway? You know what I mean? Can anybody even define it? On top of that, who listens to it? It's all bullshit. Not the music, you understand. I respect jazz. I know who Nell Carter is, okay?"

Nell Carter? Is this woman for real?

"D'you mean BETTY Carter?"

"No, yeah, whatever. But I mean, the point is that I'm not some sheltered Okie who doesn't know what jazz is. It's just, I also happen to know what it ISN'T. You know, you come to me and say, *'I'm a jazz singer,'* I'm sorry, I gotta tell ya, to me those are just code words for pretension, honey…"

Maggie Fortune was that irksome species of woman who used every sexist term ever invented by man on her own kind, Chloe was quickly learning. Dubiously armed with the honey and the sweetie, she also surely tossed words around such as *cunt* or *bitch* if she disliked you.

"You see, dear, then I'm obligated to ask, what is that? I mean, is Bill Evans jazz? Is that what you mean? Is Miles Davis? In his later stuff? Hmmm? Hmmm? See, no Okie here. Is Kenny G? Some say yes. Some say no. It's too ambiguous. That's its problem. Do yourself a favor. Don't waste your energy in a losing market. You're too valuable a talent."

It took some shifting and adjusting of an ill-fitting logic for Chloe to realize that underneath all of this coarseness Maggie was actually attempting to flatter her.

"You wanna REALLY work? Pay some bills? Forget tryin' to be a star. Forget the original project. I mean, unless you're content to just, like, sell a couple o' ten copies or so at little coffee house gigs. But you wanna make a decent living, then I can help you. There's money to be made in casuals, sweetie. Hell, Andreas and I didn't get our house in Bev Hills by drivin' down Delusion Lane. You just gotta get yourself the right repertoire. A little Top 40, some Broadway, some standards, Motown, especially Motown and R&B for you, cuz you're a Black woman, and there's a whole selling angle out there for sistas who can shake it to some Aretha and some Martha and the Vandellas and some Labelle…"

Ooohhh, and if hearing *honey* from a woman didn't do the trick of putting Chloe's panties in a bunch, hearing *sista* from a White woman trying to "sound Black" certainly accomplished it.

"…Don't even worry about the rock repertoire. Leave that to the White boys."

Ouch! Okay, the great racial divide had now officially been kicked in and set into motion. Was Chloe really sure she wanted to get in this business and be a singer? With women like this at the helm of possible employment?

"Anyway, you do all of that and you've covered all the bases. The ones that count anyway, let's face the music. Pun intended. Hah, hah, hah. But look, I hope this has been valuable for you, and I gotta go. My husband and I audition people every day, cuz we're, like, always putting on these extravaganzas, okay? So, like, today, for example, I got hip-hop dancers at three and a contortionist at three-TEN. Don't even ask. Some AOL exec looking for some weird shit for his kid's bar mitzvah. But I mean, THAT'S what life is like right now. It's eighty miles a second, baby! But look, it was a real pleasure meeting you. You have some strong talent. And I think we could use you, but you gotta get the list together. Okay, so I'll see you next class. Good meeting you, Chloe Baptiste, Creole queen! I'm telling you, they eat that exotic shit up."

And that was Chloe's very first lesson in what a casual was. What a casual office was. As many years as she had been in Julian's company, she'd never heard the term. But new friend/tornado Maggie had managed to explain why — original projects being fine and dandy and all — getting in with casuals was at least a way of paying the rent with music instead of waitressing. And that was enough to get Chloe's attention.

Her first casual was a disaster. What had she expected? She was ill-prepared, and even Maggie the Scout couldn't recognize that just by hearing her sing in a workshop. The gig was a Depression-era Storyville theme in the backyard of some movie mogul, who had tented the tennis court, and had brought in a sparkling dance floor, and had converted the whole place into a Belle Epoque New Orleans night-spot. Maggie'd been right about putting on extravaganzas. It looked amazing! Every wall had been draped in heavy velvet and brocade fabrics, with spreads of Persian rugs and Indonesian ottomans everywhere, and Baroque chandeliers hanging from every five-square-foot of ceiling, and gaudy candelabra on every clothed table, and candles galore, and paintings and caricature posters of everyone from Josephine Baker to Django Reinhardt hanging on the walls.

There were dancers and a big band, and Chloe was the "torch singer." She showed up with charts for about ten songs, all the proper era, but none that were considered standards. They were all pretty obscure, songs like *My Kinda Love* and *Clap Yo' Hands*, which Chloe had thought would make her look hip to the guys in the band. What never dawned on her was that the band would need horn parts and thorough arrangements, not just a few copies of chord charts, if she wanted them to play tunes they'd likely never played before. Call *In the Mood*, or *It Had To Be You*, and you had no problems. They knew those songs in their sleep. Plus, she didn't really know the standard form of the tunes. Again, she thought it would make her look hipper if she worked up cool, unique arrangements to them.

The first great lesson Chloe Baptiste ever learned in the world of casuals was that it's not about you. You are not the star of any show, expected to be unique, avant-garde, cutting edge. No. These party guests, ANY party guests, want only to hear songs the way they are familiar with them. Sing it like the record, or don't sing it at all. You are basically expected to be a human juke box.

So, she stumbled through her first casual, and did take notice of the pursed smiles on the lips of the musicians, which shrunk her to immediate humiliation. She had a good enough voice and a humble enough attitude, however, that she actually got more calls from Fortune Music Events beyond that night. With each new gig, there were more and more stumbles, and even bigger lessons to learn. That she knew how to read music, and therefore could at least show up with her own charts, inappropriate though they may have been, and knew the keys to her songs, was about the only thing that kept her off the shit list of the musicians she was working with. And Chloe diligently made sure to take notes and learn from her mistakes, if she wanted to keep working. In no time at all, her song list went from ten songs to twenty to fifty.

And from that moment forth, Chloe Baptiste no longer lived her whole life for Julian Troupe. She was a singer. She could rightfully call herself so, because now she actually got paid for it. It wasn't about to take her to stardom, just as Maggie Fortune had promised, but she had no reason to believe that back then. She was still wide-eyed and hopeful that she might just get to be the next Diane Shur.

Now, ten or so years later, with a repertoire inching up near three-hundred, she is considered one of the pros. She is no longer looking for a record deal. She is content to produce her own, as the independent market is now alive and thriving and threatening to bankrupt the major labels anyway, the contemplation toward which she feels some pretty wicked pleasure. But even that wonderful feeling that comes from taking your fate in your own hands comes at a price. With bills to pay, she's found herself using all of her energy keeping the Top 40 repertoire that keeps her employed updated, rather than sitting at the piano and creating Chloe's music. Julian has helped a great deal in that area, offering to assemble his very own ensemble to back a recording project he's helped Chloe launch. But like everyone else out there, it's a project that gets shoved to the back burner anytime something else comes up. Julian will hit the road for a tour, or she'll get a list of song requests from Fortune Music that's she got to shed for an upcoming event. Or she'll be reminded that it's just too hard any longer hiring musicians out-of-pocket, and going into showcase rooms, and spending money on fliers and a mailing list, and praying that people show up, because it's the only way anybody's getting paid for the gig, and making all the phone calls possible to get press there to review you, and nine times out of ten not succeeding in getting anyone there, and banging your head against a wall as you see fourteen-year-olds with boob jobs suddenly popping up on the tube with big contracts and hit songs, and here you are at forty, still trying to maintain some kind of artistic integrity by writing meaningful music. And who gives a shit! When it's just so much easier to book a bar mitzvah, show up, sing, and go home with a paycheck.

Still, she musters every bit of energy she can to avoid feeling burned out, and every so often has to remind herself that it still is a nobler living than phone sex or selling used cars.

The musicians she works with like and respect her. And this is one impenetrable Boy's Club. Their respect is important to her, except that she can't ever quite shake the suspicion that they only befriend her because she is the girlfriend of the hottest session guitarist in L.A.; a musician they all either envy, hate, admire, or are in simple celebrity awe of. And by their mere association with Chloe, they are "in" with Julian. They've probably, in most of the guy's cases, met him at various barbecues and backyard jam sessions, and now consider him their friend.

Of course, they have no earthly idea that Julian hates every last one of them. Not them as individuals, but what they represent. They do casuals. Which means, according to Julian, that they are about compromise. And making music of a certain level of integrity simply can not be a consideration, when there are worlds other considerations that have to come first, in order to make some client's party go as the fairy tale tells it.

It also means that Julian holds a certain contempt for his own girlfriend, who has not only been successful at making a workable living at casuals, but has, as well, assembled for herself a community of friends, whom she holds as deeply abiding.

And last night was the last straw. She barely got through her potential nightmare of a gig by the seat of her pants, and thankfully made it out alive, no thanks to Julian. She never did find a guitar player, after DeVoe bailed. Instead, she ran through the alternatives in her head, just so the body count would be what the client had ordered. *Some goddamned way to approach music!* she thought with great disgust. She already had a horn player, so she decided to start calling percussionists. There was a greater chance one of them might be off on a Saturday night. *This way, we can focus on a lot of the Latin and Salsa stuff,* had been her rationalization, and what she hoped the client would buy, hook, line, and sinker.

She finally managed to get Raz Emery. *Thank God! And no thanks to you, you fucking Judas DeVoe!* (Never mind what she was feeling about her own boyfriend.) Raz is a true goofball, a solid percussionist who also plays drum set, and a grateful memory of last night. She owes him big time. Especially because he gave her one of her very few laughs on an otherwise nerve-wracking job. As she recalls the moment, she laughs again, as she did last night. At the end of the gig, as Raz was tearing down his hardware, she noticed him wearing one goatskin work glove on his right hand.

"What's that glove for?" she asked.

"Well, let's just put it this way," he offered, "it's about the closest I'll ever be lucky enough to get, to havin' my way with a goat."

Even at this present instant, while drying off from her long stall-tactic shower, she laughs. It reminds her that in spite of all the crap she went through yesterday, she does indeed love working in the community of musicians that she is a part of. As in the case of Raz, it is largely a world of adults who barely rate as adults, and yet you won't find another group of people more deeply in love with what they do for a living. Even if the means to the end isn't always what they would have it be. And, as she is now having to reexamine the wrinkle-browed, humorless posturing of her own boyfriend, and his debilitating presence in her life, she finds that little bit of Peter Pan syndrome to be a very comforting thing indeed.

TRISTAN

He barely gets Anna dropped off without incident. The incident in question might've been a strangling. She does this every time, which Tristan should be flattered by, but his head and ears, already taxed from high-decibel gigging, only ring with a fury.

As soon as they'd gotten in the car to go back home to Mommy's, Anna began the solid thirty-minute screaming fit, which turned her bright pink face blood-red, induced a coughing fit, and a complete tuning out by Tristan.

It never abates. She has amazing zest for one tiny body. And he usually can't wait to get her passed off like some relay baton. He truly loves his little angel. But tantrums like those, which are clockwork for drives back to Mommy, test his will. Today especially, since his will is inconstant at best.

Graham finds his own way home whenever he feels like it, compliments of a '66 bug Tristan bought on auction and fixed up for Graham's last birthday. And besides, as far as Tristan knows, Graham is still out signing contracts and likely celebrating with his buds and forgetting all about dad. It's what kids do.

Tristan barely has it in him to do this thing for Hayes today, but there isn't even a question of whether he'll make it. This is for Hayes, damn it.

And for a moment, in this already burdensome day, he feels caressed by the quiet of his drive out of the Santa Clarita Valley and back into the San Fernando. He listens to a little Santana, and is hypnotized by the brown mountains around him that will shortly be draped by the growing tract communities. In the spring they're green and lush.

He turns from Sand Canyon onto the 14 Freeway South, and remembers the days of living in this community. Everyone he knows has made a sojourn to the outskirts in every direction, because it is in the outskirts that a musician can actually afford to buy a house on the living that is his. Santa Clarita, Rancho Cucamonga, Chino Hills. He even knows guys who drive in from Riverside just for a hundred-twenty-five dollar gig. The only ones who can afford the Westside are the ones who have lucked upon big tours or regular movie and TV dates. Most are living in suburbia.

The desolation of the Antelope Valley Freeway makes it seem wider than it actually is, and the swayed valley of freeway before him allows him to see every inch of traffic for miles. Every time he makes this trek, he drives back with a quietude that drudges up every loathing he'd begun to have for this place. His ex tells him it's different now. With new tract communities springing up, and the expansion of the Valencia Town Center, and movie and mini-mall outlets sprouting like weeds, she actually has the nerve to call her town a bustling metropolis. It is hardly that. But she assures him (surely in an effort to defend her decision to remain, when he long ago got out) that it's no longer the town he'd grown to hate.

He remembers one Halloween in particular, when he and Lisa decided to stay home and they'd entrusted Graham, then about eleven, to go circle the neighborhood with his buddies. They were friends with all their neighbors, so they knew Graham would be safe. The evening was theirs. They put *Young Frankenstein* on the VCR and were manned and ready with bowls of candy. About midway through the evening, after the umpteenth visit from children in costume, the doorbell rang again, and Tristan and Lisa welcomed yet another group of masked giggles. The tiniest little tyke in a skeleton shroud caught Lisa's eye, who promptly asked, in baby voice, "and what are you dressed as?" Little tyke answered, in barely formed words, "a dead niggah."

Tristan remembers storming out past the masks to the group of parents waiting by the curb, to demand to know who this kid belonged to, who couldn't possibly have known what he was saying, who had obviously picked it up from someone older. But Lisa pulled on his arm, begging him not to make a scene and forever mar their peace in the neighborhood.

He obliged that night, but forever after wondered what kind of woman he'd married who was more interested in keeping the neighborhood tidy than in knowing what kind of racist rednecks she was living next door to. He didn't want his kids to grow up around that.

But years later, after Anna was born and the marriage had fallen apart, he realized he hadn't much say in the matter, since Lisa had been granted primary custody, and had bought him out of their home. Any judge in the land will side with the children's home life not being upset. So, Tristan moved as far away from Canyon Country as he could, without being too many freeways away from his kids. Encino would do. The house he bought with the buyout money is half the size of the one he'd bought with Lisa. Whatever. He's a single man, now. He's got a civil enough relationship with his ex. And his kids love to visit dad. He really doesn't have a whole lot to complain about.

As he passes under the overpass from the 5 Freeway and looks up at its spindly rail, he remembers the Northridge earthquake. He was still married and living here, more than ten years ago now, when the quake completely destroyed the overpass he was now driving under, and no one could get into town for days. After that, it was another three weeks of traveling twelve miles north (the opposite direction!) to access

Angeles Crest Highway, if you wanted to get into L.A. proper. That ended up being about a four-hour drive. It was a great ruinous time for musicians. Not only because of gigs being cancelled in the wake of the immediate disaster, but because after such a calamitous thing that rocks an entire community, it's a very long time before anyone's in the mood to throw parties again. And parties are Tristan's living. Same thing happened after 9/11. The nation was in mourning. Who feels appropriate celebrating anything? It put casual musicians out of work in a devastating way.

Imagine that your livelihood depends on the frivolity of people. What does that say about your legacy? What is it actually contributing to, culturally speaking? This life you've dedicated yourself to? Tristan's ability to make a living relies solely on the smoothly running contentment of a society, so that there will always be parties to throw and merriment to make. He marvels at the oddness of that perspective. It isn't exactly repulsive, as much as perverse. And with perverse, there is always cringing, followed by a weird enticement, followed by more cringing, and the inability to reconcile a dubious moray.

He reaches for his cell phone to call Graham, when he realizes that he didn't even share the news of Graham's record deal with Lisa. Is he really that loathsome and bitter and envious? Or couldn't it have simply been that he wanted Graham to be able to break the news to his mother the way he had with his father? Tristan saw how much fun it was for Graham to spring it on him. Can't it just be that? Or is he going to have to face the petty, jealous man that he actually has the potential to be? He loves his son! But how many times has he had to say that to himself in the past twenty-four hours? Who exactly is he trying to convince?

He often thinks about the life he might have if he'd made it big in the business. If he'd had the career that Lavery Snow ended up having. In his fantasy, a reel that runs constantly, as

though there is still the chance, small irritations that break up
the Zen flow of his idyllic life, such as dropping his kid off at
his ex's, or attending the fundraiser for a dying friend, those
little inconveniences just don't ever seem to be a part of the
fantasy. Does Lavery Snow, in between power meetings at the
Ivy and red carpet events at the Kodak Theatre, have kids that
he has to chauffer back to mom's? Does he bother with old
friends who are potentially dying from transplant failure and are
plum broke? Can he still live amongst the populace that was
once his, before fame struck him?

Because Tristan wonders if he could. Or would. And he is
suddenly hit with a resentment of his day. A profound sense
that his life is mundane.

Shame shrouds him. And he realizes that he deserves his
life. A life that should be appreciated because he still makes
music and gets paid for it. Because he has two children who are
turning out to be extraordinary human beings. Because he owns
his own house and thankfully has an ex-spouse situation that is
fairly amenable. Because he has friends he can count on, who
are all artists. And because he doesn't even know any of this.
Not truly. And he deserves his life because he would be the
worst candidate ever for fame and fortune. It would make him
forget. It would make him Lavery Snow. And, in fact, he seems
to be doing his level best to forget even now, by coveting
everything else. He deserves his life so that he can be slapped
straight and told to look at his riches, have his nose shoved in it,
like dogs, when they are bad.

A surge of self-disgust moves his hand to the stereo knob
instead of the phone, and he pops in a Hendrix CD, blasting the
volume until he can't hear his own thinking. Best, really.

And if he doesn't know much else about the truest motives
behind his dubious feelings on his son's great fortune, he does
know that he would be heartbroken if Graham ever turned out
that way.

Graham is about to become surrounded by wheelers, dealers, posers, and money men. And it'll be up to Tristan to make sure Graham remains the humble kid he was raised to be. That's what Tristan can do to count in this life. Groom his son for greatness with grace. A greater grace than would've been his if he'd been given the same chances.

As he sails into the San Fernando Valley, *Fire* splitting his already compromised eardrums, he thinks for a minute that it might've actually gotten a few degrees cooler, but once you pass the hundreds, ten degrees is hardly felt. The air conditioning in his V6 engine pumps a merciful amount of Freon, but drags his SUV along more sluggishly than usual. And Tristan feels like driving fast.

When did it actually begin? This contempt he's developed for the easy fame of youth? The dichotomy is interesting to him, because the standard for quality in the recording industry has both improved, with the advent of technological advances, and at the same time plummeted to a whole new bottom, ever since the back alley, four-track recordings of rap's hall-of-fame tunes (tunes?) became a vogue and set a precedent. Any poor kid in the hood can now record some sonically shitty tracks in his bedroom, and instantly energize a culture.

Tristan understands the early frenzy of rap. It was an urban poetry that harkened, in the mind of this aging hippie, back to the beat days of Ginsberg and Kerouac, and which spoke of the struggles of a demographic that wasn't being represented in any art form. He really does understand its original appeal. It was born out of a respectable hunger. But it is far away from that hunger now. Completely out of touch with that hunger, in fact. It is now fed and kept alive by greed and money and the glitz of what they call ghetto-fabulous. Guys who grew up with silver spoons are now dumbing down their language, and trading in one set of designer wear for a new urban one, replete with bling, and manufacturing themselves into "poor kids from the hood," in order for their rapping to have credibility. The corporatizing of every nook and cranny of this culture, including its counterculture, has bled the passion to create something from scratch, from the soul, from somewhere deep inside that can't be marred, right out of the playing field.

If Tristan asked his son this minute what drove him to rap, the kid would offer up profit margin stats, and urban demographics, and fantasies of buying his parents the dream houses they have each always wanted, and money, and money, and money. Oh, and maybe women. Cuz you can tap a lot o' ass when you're Snoop.

What he wouldn't hear from Graham is, "because there is no choice," "because it stirs my soul," et al.

And then he realizes he's never actually asked those questions to Graham. This is all just a matter of arrogant assumption. In fact, there isn't much in the way of intimate conversation that ever transpires between Tristan and his son. It's a guy thing, perhaps, but men show it, not speak it. They demonstrate with action, not elaborate with words. They are not about the indulgent process, but about the quick and absolute resolve. They are articulate and eloquent in ways that have nothing to do with the English language. No one says, "I love you." They just show up when needed, and never fail to protect. The shirt off their back, always. But a heart-to-heart on the stirrings of artistic passion? Who is anyone kidding?

But if he's really going to be honest with himself, he has noticed. Tristan has watched Graham throw down his rhymes. He's peeked in when Graham and his crew are messing around on Graham's four-track, and sampling loops, and assembling sounds. He sees the fire his kid has for his effortless ability at free-form, where you rap right off the top of your head, on any given subject, and still assemble rhyming couplets with some semblance of aplomb. He does see it. Damn it, he does.

His son is connected to something, Tristan realizes in this

instant. He's been so busy moping that his son didn't walk the same tired road his old man walked, nor kicked the same rocks of frustration, that he hasn't even bothered to really see what makes his son tick. What Graham is connected to may not be something that one studies in music school, a geek's academia, but it does require the development of chops and relentless practice. Just as a drummer drills paradiddles, just as a piano player runs through endless scales, just as a woodwind player circular breathes, all to develop facility of hands and proper technique and manual dexterity and breath and a harmonic and rhythmic ear, so does Tristan's son, the rapper, hone his skill with words, to be able to group them, within an instant, into the offering of an idea, a theme, or, if nothing else, just a good old-fashioned iambic pentameter.

Now, as to whether the honing of chops will ever transcend beyond craft and into art, into the creation of something powerful, an elevated thought, is yet to be discovered in his son. Graham has every chance to be a masterful poet.

And even that! Why is *poet* a much more acceptable word to Tristan than *rapper*? He really does refuse to give it credence, doesn't he?

He has now made the transition from the 5 Freeway, through Pacoima, to the 170, through North Hollywood, and on his way into Hollywood Proper for the benefit. When the 170 becomes the 101, and he passes Universal Studios, he glances to his left, and remembers. He did a Dixieland gig there once, playing banjo and wearing a straw hat and a red and white striped blazer, which made him look like the Good Humor Man. The quartet wasn't on any stage, just strolling a designated area. He remembers. Lisa and the kids (Anna was an infant, Graham probably twelve or so) met him at the park, so they could go on rides and then stroll by and see Dad work. But Dad was embarrassed to have his kids see him looking like some goof in dress-up. Anna was enchanted by the tuba, and kept wanting to reach out and touch it. Graham just kept looking the other way.

As a kid, Tristan used to think about how awesome it would be to have a father who was a musician. Imagine if your dad was Chuck Berry. How cool would that be? Tristan's dad worked for DuPont. A company man in button-down shirt and tie clip his whole life. So, when Tristan decided that music was the life for him, he couldn't wait to have a son of his own, so that that son could have the reality that had always been Tristan's fantasy. And on the one occasion that seems to unmercifully stick out more profoundly than all the others, as he strummed his banjo with a tuba player, a clarinetist, and a drummer on marching snare, his only son was doing his antsy best not to be associated with the four dweebs in the ice cream coats.

Before the bitter memory is even done, he is long past the Lankershim exit that does this to his brain every time, and is now pouring out into Hollywood Bowl traffic and passing the Hollywood & Highland complex. The congestion of this city undoes him every time. Thank God for quiet, suburban Encino. Hollywood makes him crazy. The town *and* the symbol. But he is here to pay tribute to a great man. A man who needs to be on his feet and plucking a splendid bass again soon, so that the world is no further deprived of Hayes DeWitt's music.

Tristan is in town quite a bit earlier than he needs to be, so stops in at Amoeba Records on Sunset and Cahuenga.

"Graham, it's Dad," he says into his cell phone, finally having the nerve to call and find out what happened at the record exec meeting. But he's only leaving a message. Of course Graham doesn't answer. The Lavery Snow syndrome is probably already being set in motion. He may never be able to reach his son again.

"Haven't heard from you. Just wondering if everything went well with the paper signing. Makin' sure they didn't try to spring any new clauses on you, or anything. Mitch Williamson is good

people. If you let him conduct things, he'll get you and your
buddies what you need. Anyway, I'm not sure what you've got
goin' afterwards, but if there's the remote chance you're not
hangin' with the fellas for the rest o' the day, maybe think about
swingin' by the Union for Hayes's thing. There'll be some good
playing today. Wide array, I imagine. There might even be
somethin' you'd like—" Tristan laughs. "—and besides, it's just
a good cause for a great musician. I've played you some o'
Hayes's music before, haven't I? I'm at Amoeba right now. I'll
see if I can find somethin' of his for you to add to your
collection. Listening to this guy'll teach us all a thing or two
about music. Anyway, just checkin' in, seein' how it all went.
I'm sure it went without a hitch. Just bein' a dad. Alright, I'll talk
at'cha later. I'm on the cell all day. Oh, by the way, don't forget
to call your mother. I didn't tell her anything, I figured you'd——
" CLICK. Beep. And dead.

It always takes it out of Tristan whenever he can't get a full
thought out before the beep. It's like he should call back and
finish the sentence. But he also doesn't want to sound too
desperate for someone who's talking to a voicemail. So, he
leaves it alone, and scours back in his mind over every word just
uttered, to make sure he sounded supportive and excited and
concerned. All of which he is, even if he's having an especially
humdrum day.

As he walks into the vast warehouse of new, used, and rare
recordings from every culture and walk of life (this is Tristan's
favorite store), he thinks about the music his band, the Tristan
Baylor Project, will be offering today, in tribute to Hayes. A
couple of tunes off their just-released CD, and an arrangement
of one of Hayes's more signature compositions. Signature
enough to have made it into the Real Book. And one he's
thinking about keeping in the repertoire, even though it was
arranged especially for this event and Tristan's group tends only
toward originals. But why not? *Gilead* is a great tune.

Thinking about music helps the doldrums. Not quite as much as making it, but in an hour or so he will be. He'll be part of an all-day music-making event by musicians playing just exactly the kind of music they're feeling. In an environment surrounded by others whose entire lives are music and therefore will be listening. Will be tuning in. Will be critical. Will be exalting. Will be all the things the experience was always meant to be. Not playing some done-to-death Motown, rock, and lounge dinosaurs. Not being treated like the hired help, and reprimanded for fraternizing with the guests. And not for an unappreciative audience that really only has you there for ambiance and social status. His favorite audience is an audience of musicians, because only a fellow player can really hear the music the way it was intended.

Or is that just rationalization for all the times the layman has come up to him at club gigs and professed to not getting his music? Or asked what it is?

Did Tom Waits ever go through this? Or Sun Ra? Or any of the ones who remained on the fringes even after their fame, because their music is just so outside of categorization. A place Tristan would never mind. He just wants an "in."

He walks out of Amoeba with a handful of CDs, and heads over to the Union. He's still quite early, which means that when he arrives the tent is still being set up, catering trucks have blocked the only entrance for him to be able to unload his gear, and the stage is strewn with techies setting up the sound system and the backline. Looks like this is going to be big. In the meantime, he has to find a way to get his Explorer as close to the stage as possible, so he doesn't have to hike several blocks with three heavy guitars and his pedal board. This is going to be a nightmare load-in, with chaos abounding. He can already feel it.

But he also feels an electricity. An anticipation of a great event. A day of making great music to honor a great musician.

Hayes deserves this, and more, for his life's work.

A smile crosses Tristan's creased face, as he is reminded just how much a soother of the beast music truly is. And that he is an integral part (however small) of the collective soothing of that beast.

CHLOE

Thank God Seth let her off the hook from telling Julian that she's leaving him, by insinuating that it would not be good to stir any trouble today, with the benefit only a couple of hours away. Thank God, because this way she doesn't have to claim cowardice as the reason. She has the permission to avoid.

Julian has spent the greater part of the morning locked in his studio, anyway, while she's been bopping around watering plants and answering emails. He actually makes avoidance easy.

"You comin' to the gig later?" Julian asks over lunch, and the first time they've really seen each other today.

Chloe's brow wrinkles in confusion.

"Julian, Hayes's benefit is today."

"Yes. I know."

There is an annoyance in Julian's voice that says, *"don't ever insinuate that I'm an idiot and don't know my commitments."* Or does Chloe now simply read rudeness into every gesture, every nuance? This relationship is over. She knows it. Even if she can't quite tell him, yet. And she shames to the acknowledgement that it will help her move into it, then beyond it, if every gesture and every nuance of his contains a little venom.

"I'm talking about later tonight? Catalina's?"

"Oh, shit, yes, I'm sorry, I forgot."

"Why do you seem so distracted? You okay?"

"Well, I mean, you know. Hayes." She sprinkles a little annoyance on her own comment. And shames once again that she would use her sick friend as the excuse for her distraction.

"I mean, it's…just sad." And yet continues to do so.

"Of course," Julian says, gently placing a hand on hers. There is, all of a sudden, tenderness. *Don't do it, Julian. Don't suddenly be a saint, when I need to break away from you.*

But it wouldn't take a stretch for Chloe to realize that in all of this exchange, Julian never once asks her how the gig went last night, or if she ended up pissing off the client for a blunder he wouldn't even help her out of. It wouldn't take a stretch to realize that he was far from being a saint.

They sit at the Moroccan oak table that is a strutting peacock of a kitchen centerpiece, and states everything about what is important to Julian. Beauty, sure. Purity. But only in aesthetic things. Only in artfully crafted collectibles, or signed and numbered lithographs, with which their house is littered. Or music. Always music.

Humans, feelings, the heart. Those annoying little pests are another story altogether for Julian.

He is a Buddhist. But he can't be a very good one, Chloe thinks. She doesn't know squat about Buddhism. Other than something a friend of hers once described as the materialistic wing of the religion. There's always a black sheep. And of the many wings, Tibetan, Zen, Theravadan, that meditate for peace of spirit and for enlightenment, this particular one chants for prosper. And of course, this is the wing that Julian has been a dedicated follower of for years now. Hence, all the *things*, Chloe notes, as if she actually believes in the power.

At best, Chloe is a lapsed Baptist, who used to annoy her mother for referring to a steady church gig she once had as "going to her gig" instead of "going to church."

"But Mom, it IS my gig. I'm not a member of that church. I just have a job there."

Chloe has never felt anchored to any precept. She might've said differently at one time, if asked. In choosing to dreadlock, on Julian's behest, she chose to let her graying hair, previously always camouflaged under a hair-straightening relaxer and a good Clairol rinse, bloom forth defiantly. In giving up meat, at Julian's behest, she chose to say with self-righteous conviction that she was no longer a part of the culture that kills other living creatures. Never mind that only last week she doused the kitchen counters in Raid to eradicate the summer ant problem.

She has taken on someone else's religious beliefs because she has none of her own. Her sense of style, same story. Even her commitment to music, and this is her greatest fear, might just be someone else's.

"I'll be there," she says, stomach knotting. "You'll put me on the list?"

"Please, are you kidding? No woman of mine ever has to pay to hear me play. You are always on the list."

He is powerful in his tricks to keep her reeling. *Shake it off, Chloe.*

It's so easy for her to feel significant when someone brilliant is proudly claiming her. Like a trophy. A prize. Something inanimate and shiny. Something to put on the mantle and show off for company.

Her stomach knots even tighter, until she cannot even finish her food.

Julian gets up from his green tea and his paper, leans over to kiss her — *he feels so lovely!* — and heads to the living room for his afternoon meditation.

"You joining?"

"Maybe later," Chloe says, unable to untangle her intestines, like an irritating mic cord at a gig she's already late for. He smiles her way, and leaves her alone in their spectacular kitchen, to disappear down the hall.

She is gripped in self-doubt and held steadfast to the kitchen chair, a high-backed, oaken, carved monstrosity that is almost too heavy to scoot in and out from the table. Everything in this room is too majestic for it. She's never realized until this moment that this is the dynamic that defines Julian's very being. Everything that belongs to him screams its large significance. Including her. Because he has shaped her that way. She is only the vocalist she is, who rises above the others in the eyes of her male counterparts (save singer for the chicks musicians hate) because Julian made her so. It is Julian who compelled her to search deeper into her expression to discover the greatest music she is capable of creating. And somehow resentment *and* gratitude rise from the floorboards to confuse her and to fight for the position of primary emotion. She exists, as a human being of statement, because of Julian's molding.

Who will she be without him? When the moment comes, who will she be? And who would she be today if he had never come into her life? She begins to seethe when she recognizes that Julian would be just exactly who he is today, if she'd never come along. And she seethes at him, though she knows it is her own weakness of character that is the real culprit.

Who is Chloe Baptiste if not the woman her man is creating? Even now, as she peels through thoughts that repulse, she fears the answer might just be…no one. And if that is true, then to give up Julian is to give up herself.

She stares at the Spanish tiles that drape the wall behind the porcelain sink, and the copper pots that hang from an awning above the massive chopping table. She lives in an Architectural Digest wonderland that she has often taken credit for, with numerous *thank-you*'s to the compliments that come in droves from party guests, when she didn't have a thing to do with it. Julian made an obscene amount of money several years ago, after touring with Miles Davis on one of his last tours, and making fortuitous investments, and he bought this house when the market was at its most rape-able, and decorated every last bit of it, himself.

But it is everything that defines Chloe. It is everything she places her pride in. Frankly, she's scared to death of what will happen to her if she gives all of this up. The home that defines her. The man who completes her. The music that someone else created and mercifully attached her name to.

No, that's not true! she almost yells aloud.

But she's afraid to travel that thought any further for fear that it just might be. *Think about it, Chloe.* Though she has always written her own music (*music and lyrics,* thank you, for which she holds a kind of vain pride, because singers just aren't known for being able to compose a whole tune all by themselves), the production values that Julian has put into this current project of theirs has made it sound like him. There *is* a Julian Troupe sound, just like there's a Pat Metheny sound, or a George Benson sound.

What there is NOT is a Chloe Baptiste sound, she realizes only in this brittle instant. She is a Julian Troupe creation. Like Henry Higgins's Liza. Or Frankenstein's monster.

What she wouldn't give to be one of those sassy sapphires who knows exactly who she is, snaps her finger in the air, claims her liberation with an, "oh, no, you didn't!" marches to the bathroom (a lovely, all-white confection with Dutch linens and expensive soaps), stares into the mirror, grabs a wad of locks, and, with a pair of scissors, begins doing away with every influence that has ever been Julian's. The problem with the fantasy, however, is that if she keeps advancing the reel long enough she finds that with each snip of the sheers, not only do dreadlocks, but clumps of her very person, begin to fall away to the white marble tile, until she is the invisible woman.

She can't do this. She can't leave him.

She walks quietly down the hall and up to the doorway that leads to their living room, and watches Julian on his knees, eyes closed, sitting on the backs of his feet, hands resting, palms up, on his thighs. He sits on a meditation mat, with a zafu resting under his buttocks. From the kitchen she'd already heard the three clangs of the singing bowl that signify that meditation is now in session. It is kind of like a way, Julian once described to her, of the mind telling itself, *do not disturb*. That a rite has begun. She has often joined him, but her mind is a constant barrage, and she has never been successful at calming it. She always fidgets. Her knees begin to ache. She feels every tickle, every itch. She can never just sit still.

This late morning she watches him. He doesn't fidget. He doesn't stretch to get a kink out. He barely even breathes. He is the epitome of focus. He is with meditation as he is with music. And suddenly she doesn't feel so flippant about his spiritual practice. It's easy to toss it off as commercial, materialistic, shallow, because it doesn't identify with her. But as she watches him, she suddenly knows it is much more. In all the years she has observed his practice, and even made half-assed attempts to participate, she has never felt until this moment that there was anything much deeper than the material that he seeks. But there is. And he's obviously found it, she thinks in this instant. This is why he is such a remarkable artist. *This is why I am not.* He's connected. To what, she has no clue. But it doesn't matter. He's found his. She hasn't.

What does it take? she suddenly demands of the walls that surround her. What tapped Maria Callas on the heart and told her to sing, or else? What nudged Billie Holiday, and wrung a sublime music from that abused body and destroyed voice? Were there Julian Troupe Svengali's in these women's lives, or did theirs come from something deeply embedded inside that no man can quantify for them? And, of course, Chloe already knows the answers to those questions. What she doesn't know the answer to is this: Is she willing to risk walking away for the possibility that her passion to make music might just choose to stay back with Julian, like a child choosing a parent in divorce? After all, he is the only force that has ever given her vague aura of a musician any solid matter.

She feels suddenly unworthy to call herself a musician, a

term constantly debated as to its appropriateness in labeling a singer, anyway. She can't even count how many times she has been "corrected" by non-musicians when she says that she's a musician and is asked what instrument she plays.

"I sing."

"Oh, I thought you said you were a musician."

Do they not get that the voice is an instrument? That if I am a maker of music, then I am a musician?

She has declared that often and indignantly. But today she feels undeserving of the title. Undeserving to sing a song artfully crafted, undeserving even to stand up before a crowd of every musician in town, which she'll be doing in just a couple of hours, to honor a man who is, like Julian, the real thing, when she may, in fact, be a fraud.

She starts to cry, and quickly tiptoes out of the room, so that she doesn't alert Julian to her spying.

She walks into their bedroom, and closes the door quietly behind her. What do Hayes DeWitt and Julian Troupe have that make them do what they do so exquisitely?

She loves that her associations have always been with great artists. And she has to remind herself, during this episode of self-disgust, that Julian isn't responsible for every single musician she calls friend. Hayes isn't in Chloe's life because of Julian. In this case, it's the other way around. Chloe knows Hayes from casuals. He is a legendary thrill on the bandstand. Loves flirting with Chloe, though it's always harmless, as he is old enough to be her father, and with never any intention other than to generate smiles and a light-hearted moment. He is the kind of old school gent that would never survive in a room full of feminists.

The truth is, Hayes and Julian have never actually worked together, at least to her recollection. But there is mutual regard. The kind that has eluded her for years. Julian's ears will always prick up if she happens to mention that Hayes will be on a gig of hers.

"For once, you'll get a chance for some real playing tonight."

She has always hated comments like that. Because even though she knows he means them as compliments of Hayes, they always seem to contain, as well, this constant debilitation of her very existence.

But that Hayes is her friend more than Julian's puts just the tiniest upturn on her mouth. As if she's gathering every evidence she can of a life outside of Julian's influence.

It also makes her wonder with just a little annoyance why Seth was so disappointed when she inferred on the phone earlier that Julian might not make it today. If there was no Julian Troupe, would she have even been asked to participate? They all buddy up to Chloe to get to Julian, don't they?

Then she realizes she's gone into a completely paranoid meltdown. She rummages through her closet to pick out just the right outfit for a hot summer's day event (which they need to leave for fairly soon), and knows good and well that Seth respects her as a musician, with or without Julian's hovering presence. She's gone a little insane this morning, from being unsure if she can do this thing: Tell Julian it's over. Walk away. Pack her bags. Leave her familiar. Find a new identity. Preferably one named Chloe.

She can no longer bear up. She collapses on the bed she's only just made, still wrapped in her shower robe, though it's late in the day. Julian gave her a look earlier (though never a word) about her staying undressed all day. To him, it is such an improper ritual, in a home of many despotic rituals. Like never disturbing his wine collection, or placing his records and CDs out of their intended order and category. Or never using his meditation zafu and mat for just lying around on, while watching television. In fact, never watching television, which Chloe has learned to do only when he is not around.

"Television destroys brain cells."

She doesn't necessarily disagree. But she just wants a life of some levity. Something that, just once in awhile, is silly and unengaged in a constant wash of wrinkle-browed profundity. Something that gets allowed to follow no rules. To just be. There is no such release for Julian.

But some of us are only human.

So, a little defiance today, symbolized by the lingering in her state of undress, says that she is gearing up for a mutiny. Granted, it is a cowardly, textbook passive-aggressive mutiny.

But it's a mutiny, nonetheless.

SETH

The room smells of death. It reminds Seth of hospital rooms, where decaying flesh and rubbing alcohol are a sharp bouquet that stays with you, long after you've exited. Where the touch of the elderly and the infirmed threatens to braze your arm and remind that everything and everyone comes to their end. He fears that smell.

He needs to get Hayes up for his sitz bath, which Hayes will scream about. But Seth needs to regain some dignity to Hayes's body. When in his clearest mind, Hayes loathes the smell that emanates from a leg that is slowly rotting. And to be honest, the bath is for Seth, too. To ward off the smell of death for another day, another month, another ten years. That's what the drugs are promising. And a new slew of them that might help with the circulation in his leg are also promised, if the insurance company is willing to foot the bill, and if this benefit today can help offset the rest.

There is promise. But at the moment, that promise is being smothered by the smell. And so is Seth.

"Hayes, we need to get going. I'm gonna draw your bath for you."

"Where are we going?" Hayes asks, more passive than he's been all day. He floats in and out of a twilight sleep, and in between he attempts pages from *Beneath the Underdog*, Charles Mingus's near-biblical autobiography, which Hayes has read and re-read probably thirty times.

"Oh damn it all blues…" he reads out loud to Seth, savoring every bit of cracked poetry, *"…Screwed to the melting frozen walk of dared-to-embrace stone, concrete hard, imagined soft…"*

He puts the book down.

"You know what that means?"

"Uh…I suppose it could mean a lot o' things."

"Coward! Be bold! Seize the day! Have an opinion, goddamn it! It means that everything is a disillusion. We think this artistic pursuit of ours is somehow going to register in the history books as profound, as culture-shifting, and that we'll be viewed as these enlightened, sentient beings. These special people on earth. These deliverers. But not only is the reality NOT that romantic, it is, most essentially, a dogged trek down a dead-end, fly-ridden road. And there is where the real heartbreak lies. The true blues."

"How do you know that's what Mingus meant?"

"I don't give a good goddamn if that's what he meant. It's what I got."

And then he fades again.

Seth looks at the clock on a far wall. It doesn't really matter if the concert begins before they arrive. Actually, it's better if he can drive up with Hayes, open the passenger door for him, and have music pouring forth as Hayes looks around and wonders what's going on. That will be perfect. Of course, Hayes will gripe the whole way, because it's what he does. But Seth will be smiling inside, because he'll get to see, from his front row seat, this force that he is responsible for, this gathering of every L.A. musician to've ever made a mark on this town, shut up the ever-vocal Hayes DeWitt. And humble him. And maybe even cause him to shed a tear. To know that they've all gathered together for him. Seth smiles to imagine it, even as he looks at the clock and feels alternately hasty about getting going, and perfectly okay about lingering a tad longer.

"I don't want to go anywhere today, if that's okay with

you," Hayes utters again, but with eyes closed.

"But it's a nice day."

"It's a hot day."

"It'll do you good to get out."

"I don't want to go!" he barks.

"Okay. We won't. We don't have to go anywhere."

Minutes from now Hayes won't remember he argued. Still, it bothers Seth that this mental synapse is beginning to be a part of the daily tapestry.

"Have you ever wondered why we do what we do?" Hayes suddenly asks.

"What do you mean?"

"I mean, everything we've ever collected, acquired...all the *things*...that tell the world, that tell our friends, that, that tell ourselves where we stand on the social strata...that priceless collectible we almost got into a fist fight over at the art auction, because we just had to have it...that house in the suburbs where our kids could grow up, that we almost lost our shirt trying to buy, only for those kids to leave us anyway...that World Series where if the fucking Yankees didn't win, we just, we were just not going to be able to live any longer...that, that, that woman, that elusive woman who shined us on for years, who wouldn't give us the time of day, which ultimately just fueled us even further in the fight to get her..."

His forehead is glistening.

"...that, that, concerto we worked on for years, sometimes, that we perfected, and we fine-tuned, and we tweaked, and when it finally got played by the Philharmonic, we thought to ourselves, *'it's still not right, goddamn it,'* because we think that by changing that one note to resolve one way instead of another, we'll change the world. But the world never gets changed. It just...and it's not a bad thing, it's just...it goes in cycles, you know? And...and...and...the current cycles are always vaguely familiar to the past ones, and then you realize that art doesn't shape us nearly as much as we think it does, or should. It doesn't propel us forward. It just adds a pair of endless repeat signs. Because, as artists, we live this pink and gold idyll that says that art heals, that art transforms and transcends, that art is this great spiritual warrior against complacency and closed-mindedness and static...static...so much static..."

Seth stares into the face.

"...I didn't do it. I didn't do it. I didn't do it." Hayes weeps. Seth has never seen this. "I didn't do it..."

"You didn't do what?" Seth asks, but is afraid to utter anything. If there is a spell that can be broken by the sound of his voice, he wonders if it should be broken. Hayes is purging right now. Some deep sore that Seth has always known was hanging around like a ghost, but would never really come to the surface, except in Hayes's tantrums. But never like this.

"I didn't do, I didn't do...I didn't do...the great thing, that, that, that, that one great thing we're all supposed to do."

"What're you talking about? You've done so many great things, you can't even count."

"No, no, no, no, no! I didn't do my one great thing."

"I don't know what you mean," Seth whispers.

He hates having to tell Hayes that he isn't on this wave with him. He wants to be, so badly that his head hurts from trying to climb inside Hayes's brain right now and really get him. He wants to just say, *"I know."* But he can't. It would be wrong to agree with Hayes that he hasn't done some great nebulous thing. Hayes is the greatest man Seth knows. But it seems wrong, as well, to say, *"I don't understand."* To not be in solidarity with his flight.

Seth's whole adult life has been about getting Hayes, truly understanding the life lessons this man has bestowed upon him. He is a poor student. A failure at being Hayes's angel, right now. Because he doesn't want this flight. He isn't ready. Hayes seems to be, but not Seth.

He holds Hayes's hand and tries to pat his forehead with the sleeve of his shirt. It's the delirium again.

Hayes looks at him. Really looks at him. As if trying to connect. As if trying to remember who Seth is. But that isn't it. Seth knows that Hayes's eyes aren't betraying him. Against his own desire for Hayes to be delirious in this moment, he knows that Hayes isn't having another one of his episodes. Hayes is clear. He is speaking a language that Seth can't really understand, but he is here. Present. And it is Seth, now, who becomes the very person he, himself, has always been frustrated by.

It never seems to fail that whenever he has ever tried to share with someone his periodic feelings of isolation or claustrophobia or whatever particular struggle it is this week, they, whoever *they* are, will inevitably, hastily, reach for the quickest, nearest antidote, as though a quick fix is all he needs, when what he needs most is for an accomplice, someone with whom he can commiserate, start a club with, have a secret code of understanding that need not be exchanged in words but on a deeper level of connection. He needs their empathy, not their sympathy. He knows this. He's felt this. And right now, he is being that very friend who just wants to make it all better for Hayes. Who refuses to just commiserate.

He knows good and well that Hayes isn't looking for someone who can prescribe the miracle pill that makes it all better. Hayes is looking to sort out, to break down and dissect, to peel the layers off of a complex puzzle, in order to reach a deeper understanding of his own magnificently dubious reality. And he needs Seth to understand.

But Seth is afraid, as most people are whose instincts to offer a solution aren't really about an altruistic impulse to help, or save, or rescue. It is out of fear. It is that person's instinct for self-preservation. It is the protective mechanism that can't, won't, is afraid to have to help someone cope. To have to walk through that dank alleyway with their friend in crisis.

Seth shakes it off. He will not be that kind of friend. He will not shy away from walking that dank alleyway with Hayes. Against his instinct to say, *"it's all okay,"* or, *"you have done great things,"* against his own fear, he will walk.

He is afraid to ask it, but does. "What is this great thing that you didn't do? Because I see only great things. So, please help me understand."

"Did you know that I met Picasso once? In Paris."

Seth is exhausted from trying to keep up with a man who is only sprinting these obstacle courses to shield Seth from the intimacy of death. Hayes knows that Seth is afraid. Seth knows that Hayes knows this. And Seth is ashamed for exposing these fears. He doesn't want to walk with his friend through whatever darkness has come over Hayes with gritted teeth and trembling shoulders. But he does it. And because Hayes knows this, Hayes changes course.

"I was there playing with this singer, Ruby Chan. You ever hear of her?"

Seth shakes his head. No use even trying to bear up.

"Yeah, we partied with him in this club up in Montmartre. Fuckin' Picasso, man! I was just a young kid. Barely outta my teens. And he was already a legend. Even then, I knew that. I knew what he was, and I knew what he'd become. Anyway, he once said something I'll never forget. Not to me, like, personally, just, just…it became this quoted thing. He said, *'art is not meant to decorate walls. It is an instrument of war.'*"

"I think I've heard that one," Seth lies. He is terrible at this.

"And Gauguin once said…you know that he and Picasso were roommates in Paris, don't you? Wait a minute, no, fuck, I'm gettin' my timelines all mixed up. Gauguin was a post-impressionist. He was a-fucking-hundred years before Picasso. What the Hell am I talking about? Who am I thinking of? Oh shit, Van Gogh! That's who I'm thinkin' of. He was Gauguin's roommate. Shit, I'm losing my mind. How'd I get off on Van Gogh, anyway? What was I talking about?"

"You were about to tell me something Gauguin once said?"

"Oh yeah."

He seems ready to say it, but perhaps is mulling it over first, or savoring it, Seth can't tell which. Or maybe even in conflict with it.

Then: "*I close my eyes in order to see.*"

And then Hayes does just that. He lets out a grateful, long breath, as though he's been holding it for four minutes, and tries to smile but is stopped.

"Art meant something to those guys." His eyes remain closed. "Do you think the world's a better place because of Picasso and Gauguin?"

"Sure."

"But do you think anybody else thinks so? Or just other artists? Cuz, see, we aren't the ones who need to hear what they have to offer, so much. We already know. We already know what it means to dig so deep inside ourselves that we bring out these buried bones that illuminate the human condition, because they are the human condition, in its most honest form. It's everybody else who needs to be touched by that, who needs that kind of connection to their life. But I don't know that they are. Touched by it, I mean."

What can Seth offer?

"The reason I didn't do the great thing," says Hayes, "is because there is no great thing."

The sentence reverberates in a wash of dampness throughout the air in the stolid room. This ochre Hell. If this is wisdom talking, then Seth sinks into despair for the human race. For his own efforts his entire life.

"There is only time passing," Hayes continues. "And if you're lucky to pass it without doing too much damage to the ones you encounter, then your life is a good one. But that's the barometer. It ain't spectacular. But it's something."

This is Hayes's lifelong bitterness coming to its resolve. His statement to the world, like Picasso's or Gauguin's or even Mingus's, something to be quoted after his death, something illuminating, but far bitterer than Pablo's, Paul's, or Charlie's, who each still believed in an artful world even at their deaths, while Hayes DeWitt is concluding that all artistic effort is meaningless. It is the bleakest of his existentialist beliefs.

Seth wants to tell Hayes that that's a lie. He wants to defy him. He wants to lash out. What keeps him from it, besides the obvious, is the kernel of truth in that diatribe, the one about not damaging the ones you encounter. Seth's life might've gone the way of a whole other set of fortunes had his own dad followed Hayes's cynical but frighteningly simple barometer for a good life. Creating something great before we die is a wonderful idyll. But there is a lot to be said, as well, for simply not doing damage.

The room is suddenly small and warm. The ochre walls close in until there is only room for two sets of elbows and four clinched fists.

This isn't Hayes's time. But there is the creeping feeling in Seth that Hayes thinks it is. He just needs reassurance, that's all. The leg is going bad, sure, but it's not even to the point of being irreversible yet. There are still steps that can be taken, that are being taken. They're considering him for another heart, and have waived the fact that he just recently reached a birthday that legally makes him no longer eligible. Things are looking up, and this benefit today could do wonders, not only from the financial standpoint, but in terms of his self-worth, which seems at this moment to have plummeted to an all new low. Or is this just what happens when we're letting go? When we're saying "enough"? We excavate and we analyze, looking for a way to make it easier to let go. Looking for the loophole, as W. C. Fields once said.

If Hayes is beginning this process of letting go, it puts Seth into a frenzy that it would begin today. *Not today! Start letting go tomorrow, when you've had the chance to see how much your world loves and hails you. Because if you can see that, then maybe you won't be ready to let go. Maybe you'll fight harder. Fight, damn it!*

Seth stares furiously into a dark, sunken face, a tired life, old memories of drinking in bars with Picasso. Hayes is forty pounds lighter than a man his size and height should be. This great man who has hovered over Seth's life like Moses is suddenly small and meek. And letting go.

Seth is scared. He suddenly cannot breathe with facility. He takes deep breaths and holds Hayes's hand as firmly as a man who is trying to say, *"I love you"* can. The breaths are so rhythmic and deliberate that it almost hypnotizes him. And they stare at each other until their eyes are locked.

Father and son. Not teacher and student anymore. Or even caregiver and patient. It is beyond the pragmatic. Beyond roles. Beyond music lessons on descending cadences. Beyond prescribed medications that may or may not extend life. Beyond this house. Beyond gigs. Beyond benefit concerts. Beyond dusty reminiscences of a long life. Beyond race. They are in a place Set doesn't want to leave. An immediate here and now. The only moment that matters. And Hayes has brought them here.

NICK

His sits at the bar of the downtown Orchid Club on Eighth Street near San Pedro, nursing his fifth (sixth?) scotch rocks, and weeping over the singer on stage. He weeps a lot when he drinks. Not the kind of weeping that slobbers kisses and expressions of drooly love your way. But angry, achy weeping. Every wound is exposed when Nick Brandt drinks, and this day is no exception. Except that there is no singer on the stage at 2:30 this afternoon. The place has a few diehard regulars, but is otherwise quiet. He stares at the stage, the grand piano that is covered with a tarp, the microphone on its stand. And the empty space behind it.

He managed to finish his gig at the Ritz Huntington without getting fired for the four scotches he had sneaked in on his breaks, and was on his way into Hollywood for Hayes's benefit (he'll still make it in time), when he suddenly had an overwhelming urge.

"Where's Dorothy?" he slurs to bartender Otto. "I came to hear a great singer, cuz they are just a rare fucking breed in this town."

"Dorothy doesn't come in till later. It's two in the afternoon, mate. There's no music till tonight. And you know you're not supposed to be here, anyway."

"Man, jus' wait, jus' hold on. I'm not here to make trouble."

"Nick—"

"Naw, really, Nick…I mean, Otto—" he starts laughing.

"I'm Nick. You're Otto."

"Want me to call you a cab, Nick?"

"Naw, man, I'm fine. I got a thing later. I jus', I'm just stoppin' in. I won't be here when she shows up. I promise. I never am, am I?"

"Nick—"

"Naw, man, I'm serious. I got this thing I gotta be at. Benefit for an old friend."

"Well, you're gonna sober up before I let you drive out o' here."

"Tha's fair. I'm jus' gonna sit for a minute."

But Nick can see her up there. His imagination can conjure just about any old needed vision if he's drunk enough. There she is, singing her Ellington, which was always signature for her.

Nick wishes he could be in her piano player's shoes, instead of the ones he is presently wearing. Not because the guy on stage (who looks an awful lot like him) isn't doing her justice. The guy fucking is! In the best sense of the word. But because it would be so much less painful backing this amazing singer, who would be, with him and the rest of the trio, traveling to Heaven; instead of hanging, in a stupor, off the bar rail, with an overwhelming need to purge gut and sins. Maybe. Maybe not.

Too many singers, in this day and age, are about bullshit. Too many of them about shouting the roof off, about showing everything they've got in a single cadence, which is usually some gaudy circus of vocally acrobatic, overwrought, elaborate, melismatic crap. Usually a case of being too afraid to sustain a single, exposed, beautiful note, because someone may just discover there's no actual voice there, just this thin, reedy gimmick. Nick can spot a fraud at twenty paces. But it is even more achesome to spot the real thing.

"Goddamn, she's good," he mutters.

Otto looks in the direction of Nick's stares, the empty stage, and shakes his head.

"Yeah, she's good, mate."

Nick invariably ends up wallowing with a painful longing in
the days of doing gigs with his ex-wife. The first ex-wife. The
second one he barely remembers. Arm Candy. That's all. But
Dorothy. He wonders if Dorothy is still good. In his conjurings,
in the Dorothy chimera that stands on that stage right now,
evoking every lovely memory he's ever had, she is stunning. But
he has no way of really knowing, because she has refused
contact with him from the day he moved out of their house,
eight years ago. Something about a restraining order, which
even bartender Otto seems to know about, and a charge of
spousal abuse, which Nick refuses to give any credence to. He
never hit her! She claims it, but it isn't true.

And why? Why would she accuse him of something so
heinous, when she knows him better than anyone? Nick Brandt
is harmless. Except maybe to himself. He plays a tender piano,
fraught with fragility and poignancy. How could she possibly
think that the man who loathes a brash note would have the
capacity to wield a brash hand?

And at that thought, Nick stumbles up and makes his way
to the men's room for a piss.

"Dear God, why?" he cries, as he undoes his fly, leans his
pelvis forward, takes a leak in the urinal, and does the ritual he
does every day. Has arguments with God. Pleads with him,
badgers him, challenges him, debates him. And apparently it
doesn't matter whether Nick carries on this domestic squabble
at home or in some public restroom somewhere. He simply
paces his space—wherever that is, and today it happens to be in
some foul toilet in a downtown bar, only a block from Skid
Row—and goes round one with the Almighty.

"Why have you given me such a miserable life? I give all
glory to you, Lord, I wear out my fucking knees asking for your
bountiful blessings. I never hit her! You know I never did. She
was afraid of me because I'd get drunk. And even I was afraid

of me when I'd get drunk, but she was never in any danger. I
mighta ransacked the house once or twice, or punched a wall, or
bashed a car window. I admit those things. But I never laid a
hand on her. And that was a decade ago, anyway! Why is it
burdening me now? See, that's what you do, Lord! You play
with my head. You put things back in there that I've tried my
goddamnedest to shut out. And why? Are you s'posed to be
teachin' me some sort o' lesson? What lesson! I'm doin' my bes'
to live a pure life. I make music with no compromise. None!
And it's not that popular a position to take, I gotta tell you.
These goddamn casuals. It's like I'm sellin' my soul to the Devil,
and for what? So some asshole in power can come up to me at
the end o' the night, and pat me on the head, and say, *'you did a
good job'*? And I'm s'posed to cakewalk and gyrate and smile and
be grateful that the royals threw me a crumb? Well, I say *'fuck
you'* to that. Okay, so I don't smile for the pretty people, but I
give 'em something more important. I give 'em my heart. Which
they never fucking recognize right there in front of 'em
anyways, because they're too busy bein' insulted that I'm not
bein' their yes-boy, and gushin' about how happy I am to be
there. But I DO give 'em my heart, Lord, because I know tha's
the only way it can be done. Your own son came down from
Heaven to give the world his heart. And I am only tryin' to
follow the word of your only begotten son, Lord. And how do
you repay me for it? You plague me with bein' able to recognize
the real thing when it comes to music. The kind o' music that
transcends the spirit in the very same way that your benevolent
son did it. And because there's so little'a that kinna music bein'
made today, in this fucking cutthroat world that is wooed by
money and celebrity, you make it impossible for me to smile.
You make me hate the game, and you make everybody else hate
me. You make me the town grouch, because I can't cope with
the goddamned mediocrity out there that isn't even about some
elitist notion of who's special and who's not. It ain't about

chops, man. The mediocrity can be so easily, easily bamished...banished by, by, by jus' bein' dedicated to a pure cause. It's so easy. And yet so few musicians are, man. God, man!

"AND you make me a weakling for the juice, because you know how much better it makes everything feel jus' to be able to numb it all out and make it go away for a night. F-f-fu-u-ck ...I...c-c-ca-an't...c-c-cope. Why can't you give me any peace, Lord? I praise your name every day that I breathe, and try to give to this fucking worl' my pures' heart through this music that you've seen fit to burden me with, like a thirst I can't quench. Why did you even bother to make it so important to me? Why couldn't you jus' make me okay with all the bullshit? My life would certainly be less tormented. My own brothers, they're not tormented. Cyril is jus' so happy to sit behind a piano and play a great tune great, and smile, and bow, and shake somebody's hand when they put a buck in the tip jar. Why have you given him peace with it all, and not me? What do I have to do, Lord? Please tell me? Tell me what is thy will, and it will be done. I am happy to do your work, but you gotta give me a clear map."

Nick grows exhausted, but not before he hears a few knocks on the wall from outside the restroom, to keep it down. God, he hadn't even realized he'd been ranting all of this out loud. That's what six (seven?) scotches will do to you. He is being as socially reprehensible as Phone Lady from the airport last night. He needs another drink badly—he knows that for certain—before he'll be able to face the plethora of musicians and singers and sell-outs at this benefit shindig later.

"Have you ever heard of Hayes DeWitt?" he asks Otto, after returning to his stool at the bar.

"No, mate. Can't say as I have."

Nick is suddenly distracted by the darkness of the room. There are no windows in bars, he realizes for the first time in his life, as he replays every bar he's ever frequented in his head. They must be designed that way to give the illusion that it is perpetually nighttime, the bewitching hour of drink. Because who drinks in the strutting vainglory of daylight? No one who isn't feeding on the bottom rung. And he is comforted, cocooned even, by the darkness. And then he suddenly remembers he's in conversation with Otto.

"Yeah, well, Hayes DeWitt is, uh—he's a mother-fucker, is what that mother-fucker is. Yeah, him and me and Dorothy and this drummer, Balthazar Brava, now there's a name, right? Anyway, we used to do this quartet thing, man, no horns, jus' this sweet rhythm session, man. I mean, SEC-tion. Sorry."

Otto nods his head in acknowledgement of what Nick is saying, even as he tugs his way subtly to the other end of the bar to help another patron. Wouldn't want Nick to think he doesn't like chatting with him. But Nick doesn't even notice. Just keeps talking, from down at the other end.

"Did you know this guy played with Dizzy Gillespie?"

"Well, seein' as I've never heard o' the guy, I did not know this. But that's very cool."

"You DO know who Dizzy Gillespie is."

"Yes. I know Dizzy Gillespie."

"Yeah, well, you should fuckin' know Hayes DeWitt, too, man. And I'm not sayin' you, like, as in YOU, like it's your fault that you don't know him. I jus' mean, it's a fuckin' shame that the world hasn't hailed him enough for even any ol' bartender to know."

"Thanks, mate."

Otto knows Nick's rants right now are alcohol inspired. He knows Nick means no harm.

"Naw, man, I'm jus' sayin'—"

"I get'cha," says Otto. "So, tell me about this musician friend of yours who should be famous."

"We used to do this gig, together, man. Him and Dorothy

and this drummer and me, back in the day. It was so sweet. Those mother-fuckers know how to deliver a song. Man, Hayes's bass is jus' about the warmes', deepes' pocket…thing you ever heard. Man, that mother-fucker can swing."

"You say he's a singer, too, huh?"

"Not sing, goddamn it, SWING! What the fuck!"

"Sorry," Otto says, smiling. Nick's a handful.

"You know what it is to swing, don't you?"

"I think I've heard enough jazz in my lifetime to have an idea. Been here with Dorothy for years now."

"Tha's right. Tha's RIGHT! Your relationship with Dorothy has lasted longer than mine ever did. Once again, the key to a successful marriage proves itself to be…no sex!"

Both men chuckle at Nick's sad attempt at humor.

"Anyway, we would trade fours, man. You know what tradin' fours means?"

"No, mate, I guess I don't."

"It's when, like, after the solo section, you, like, go back over the form again, but this time everybody takes turns soloin' over four bars each, and then it's handed over to the next guy for his four bars, and it goes round and round like that till the whole form is played, and then you go back to the head. Anyway, we would trade fours, man. Dorothy, too, cuz she could improvise over the changes. She really heard 'em, you know? And every time we'd do that, it would jus' be, like, this, this, this conversation that was never rude, and would never dare to interrupt you if you were speaking. No one needed to top each other. It was a conversation, you know? Not a debate, not an argument. But a dialogue. A stanza in a poem. And each new stanza would support the last, the way couplets complement each other in a sonnet. And you would say your piece, and give way to the next man. And then you would listen to him, because he had something to say, too. And it might just take you in one direction, but then it might just take you in another. And you'd better be prepared for that. Because that's the whole beauty. This unexpected road, perhaps one yet untraveled by any human being. And there would be something serendipitous about you and your comrades being the first. And you would emerge from this courteous exchange, this dialectic of gentlemen, of regard and respect and awe, and you would rise to the occasion, because you'd know you were in the presence of greatness. And you each felt that about the other. Each relevant. There is no caste system in a moment like that. Nobody who's the leader. No alpha musician. No showing off or being so edgy that you're falling off the edge of the fuckin' earth, man. Your edge isn't conscious, it isn't something you put on, like a cloak, like vain pride. It is simply what you are, because you've dared to take a risk, trust your comrades as you would yourself…and be free."

Otto now gives Nick his full attention, who'd stopped slurring for that one. Otto isn't exactly sure what Nick is talking about, but he knows it's pure, whatever it is. Because a man sobers up when he speaks of something holy.

"That's how you're free, man. Not by winning the lottery. Not by having some beautiful woman on your arm. But by tapping into beauty. Tapping into beauty is how you're free, my friend."

He almost tears up, until he catches himself.

"That, and a shot o' whiskey."

Otto laughs.

"How 'bout a cup o' coffee instead, mate?"

Nick chuckles and wanders over to the stage, where he sits behind the piano, pulls back the tarp, and lifts the lid. There's no light on him, which is better. He doesn't really wish to be noticed. He just wants to go to that place. That place he just finished describing to Otto. That place that is as elusive as a woman's heart, but is so filled with promise, so illuminated with light, so free of worldly concern. Such as, who is willing to love him? Who is willing to forgive? And how does he get into his car right now, leave Dorothy behind, who isn't waiting anyway, and celebrate his friend, his colleague, his brother in all things music?

He places his hands on the keyboard. Thank God it's tuned. There is nothing worse than the neglect of an instrument. He's played enough gigs on out-of-tuned pianos, pianos with keys missing, strings broken. It mars the journey, to be sure. But it's also just a slap in the face to the music and the musicians who create it. How many times has he dealt with club owners who brag about the quality jazz in their establishment, yet refuse to keep their pianos in working order?

But at this moment, on a newly tuned grand, a tender minor 9th – flatted 13th has placed its massaging hand on Nick's heart, and *'Round Midnight* sings to him. Almost as beautifully as his Dorothy used to do it.

He's always been a piano player who hears the lyrics, even when the song's being done instrumentally. It's the fucking song, for Christ's sake! Guys who play a song without knowing the lyrics, without truly hearing them, are not really connected (if that's even important to them), and therefore have no clue how to interpret it, how to reflect the song's meaning from their piano work, and as a result are only giving you half the heart of it. And as any doctor will tell you, half a heart isn't going to do any body any good.

It begins to tell... 'round midnight, 'round midnight.

It doesn't take midnight to tell Nick that he is lost. It only takes three o'clock in the afternoon, an empty bar, seven scotches, and a kind soul named Otto, who now places a hot cup of coffee on the lid next to him.

I do pretty well till after sundown.

Most days that's true. Today's a hard one for Nick.

And yet a song like this, and the permission to play it with every bit of heart invested, really is the only thing that just might keep Nick from another drink and a slow, downward spiral.

CHLOE

Lying on top of their goose-down comforter (another no-no in the House of Julian; the feathers get mashed and matted), Chloe is suddenly visited by a memory of music. The days when everything in her relationship was still fresh, when every touch and gesture was interpreted and wondered at. *Did he mean to braze my fingers with his, as we were walking?* And it all had the largeness of purpose that usually only the smoking of pot can really capture so sublimely. Everything, in those early days of dating Julian, was large and breathtaking, because there was still that euphoria of the new. That's the problem with being introduced to music by someone you're sleeping with. You enter music's life in an altered state, and in that state everything sounds and feels wonderful. There is no discernment. No discrimination.

Julian hipped her to Eddie Jefferson, and to Eddie's inimitable way of using his voice like a horn, of giving lyrics and vocalise to famous bebop solos. Julian made her listen to Ella Fitzgerald, made her get inside Ella's head and ears, and hear the harmonic changes the way Ella heard them. Julian played lots of Afro Cuban music for her, and taught her all about the clavé, and how it is the very center and driving force of that culture's music. Julian inspired a hunger in her for the free-association music of Ornette Coleman and later Coltrane, and helped her plow through the seeming chaos of their acid-inducing music that was on the surface, to really hear what it was they were expressing, and that it wasn't chaos, at all. That there was actually a logical — if coming *this* close to falling off the edge — progression of ideas. And she could actually hear it. *She could really hear it!* Which gave her more of a high than she has ever experienced with pot.

But for the life of her, as she revisits those days, those life-changing moments, those moments that told her, in no uncertain terms, that she was indeed a musician and would accomplish great things, for the life of her, she can't figure out if that high, which came from being able to hear what the layman might not, was an organic fostering of a head and heart meant for music, or if she was simply reeling from the orgasm of this stimulating man, his music, his love and lust for her, and his newfound claim that his girlfriend could now speak the language he spoke, and was worthy of joining the roundtable, also known as the Boy's Club.

The Boy's Club has always been Chloe's doppelgänger. It is rare for a chick singer to be allowed entrance. Even rarer for chick players. Women players are always assumed to be weak, and when they're discovered not to be, they are suddenly a novelty, and therefore *must* be gay. Chick players are gay, chick singers are sluts. Which Chloe can't help but see as an awfully convenient prejudice, considering every man's weakness for the two-women-together scenario. She chuckles in a kind of depleted way at the inanity that is still never quite inane enough to render her unimpressed with the Boy's Club. She still wants in.

She thinks about that wake-up call she got years ago at Julian's first CD release event.

For some it is enough to nurture the greatness in others...

The summons that day had told her it was not enough. But maybe she should've been content to simply nurture the artist in Julian. Because, after all of the tutoring and apprenticing, where has it gotten her to've operated under the illusion that she is one?

There is nothing ignoble about supporting a great artist from the background. Dear poor Leonard did it for Virginia Woolf. Chan did it for Charlie Parker. Theo did it for Vincent.

But Chloe dared to be one herself, and where has it gotten her? She couldn't even land the Madonna gig to be a fucking back-up singer, when she can sing circles around Madonna.

Yet every time she thinks thoughts like that, a clot forms in the back of her throat, obstructing her windpipe, at the morbid fear that she might come off to others as arrogant. Julian doesn't suffer that problem. Neither does Hayes DeWitt. Hayes once told her, "you must have contempt for them all," when she dared to share her lament over the loss of the Madonna tour.

"Screw Madonna," Hayes had said that day, which felt so good to have said on her behalf. And thank God someone else said it, so that she would never have to appear vain, because she is incapable of the Screw Madonna mantra herself. She feels undeserving of vanity.

"Madonna's not fit to wipe your ass!" Hayes continued that day on the bandstand. But past a certain point, there begins to be discomfort. After all, Chloe doesn't really want Madonna to wipe her ass. She's much more disappointed than disgusted. Not like Hayes was. Or Julian.

But not even Julian could offer "screw Madonna" on Chloe's behalf. At least with Hayes, he was in her corner. Offering words like: "Madonna doesn't know what she passed up," and "you'd've brought some class to that operation."

At best, Julian felt it was beneath her to have auditioned in the first place, and undignified to have been so excited about the prospects a gig like that would've virtually guaranteed. No matter what he had to offer, it was always still a dig to Chloe.

"There is no purity in that."

Aagghh! Again with the fucking purity shit. Does he get that from his Buddhism?

"You know, I mean, if that's the way you want to make your legacy..."

"Damn it, Julian, it's an awesome opportunity!" she recalls from one of so many conversations like it. "Do you know how much my own project would be paid attention to, if I was one of Madonna's singers? Our CD..." (she always had to make sure to call it *their* CD, not just hers) "...could get some serious distribution with that association. Don't turn your nose up at it. Not all of us get to land gigs with Miles Davis, okay! I haven't been as lucky as you. I'm making ends meet the best way I know how. At least it's with music..."

And then she realizes that she's having this argument right now, by herself, in a room alone. This is no visitation upon a distant memory.

"...You know what? Hate casuals if you want. But I don't, okay? I have fun on them. I like the guys I work with, and they like me. Yes, sometimes I have to sing songs I'm absolutely sick of. So what! Guess what. We don't all get the chance for the brass ring that you've been handed. Try being gracious about the fortune you've been given, instead of so contemptuous of those of us who have no choice but to do what we can to stay afloat."

But what keeps Chloe from actually saying those words to Julian's face is fear of his retort. That it might just be something along the lines of:

"Brass ring has nothing to do with it. I've been given my good fortune because I don't settle. Not for a casual, and not for Madonna. The fact that you actually believe that what you're making up there on the Blitzstein wedding's bandstand is music is precisely why you will forever be a casual singer."

As if it is a death sentence for unspeakable crimes against humanity. She knows this is how he feels. She knows it will never change. And she knows exactly what she must do.

"Even Charlie Parker did casuals!" she imaginarily screams

in her imaginary argument. "So, fuck you!"

She is fueled for confrontation right now. Screw Seth's request for her to put her crucial life decision on hold for his little party. She can no longer breathe, and if she continues on in this way they'll have to throw a benefit for her.

Except that no one throws benefits for dying chick singers.

She almost moves from her lying position, until she suddenly hears the sounds coming from Julian's studio. He's done with his meditation, and is playing back the last tracks they'd laid a few days before on Chloe's CD.

Her own voice, with a little reverb added to the rough mix for listening back purposes, haunts the hallways. It is the same delicate waltz that Chloe had been listening to in her car last night, called *One of These Days*, about unrequited promises to change one's life.

She begins to be overtaken by its haunting. It is painful. The chorus continues to repeat empty promises that the listener knows will never be made manifest. And so, it is a sad song. Kind of Chloe's specialty. She wrote it a few months ago already, but now listens to it, as she lies in the hollow middle of her new quandary, and wonders how she knew, at the time she wrote it, that this little piece of fiction would become a truth for her, so shortly following. The muse taps us in elusive ways. And it is just those little phenomena at which Chloe is constantly awestruck, but actually prefers having no answers to. If they remain mystical for her, she finds that she remains respectful of them.

It's interesting to her that Julian seems to migrate repeatedly to this song, as well. If he ever bothered to pay attention to lyrics, would he even recognize the prophecy in her words? Would he realize where they came from? That something is brewing in the heart of his significant other, something she wasn't even aware of at the time she created it, and that an imminent eruption may be in the offing?

Well, then, it's a good thing Julian doesn't really give a shit about lyrics. They are simply the necessary evil that gives a singer her reason to be. Or is she now just feeling petty?

She listens to her voice. It's a sweet voice. Not void of character, but stylistically it does tend to be more neutral (she hates the word *generic*) than most singers she knows. They're usually either R&B singers, with the licks to punch up any tune, or really straight, legit singers who make her cringe on a Motown song, but who can carry the standards with relative elegance. Or her friend Dominique Wayne, who drips pathos off of every note of every song. Or Gwen Cummings, who can sing higher than Mariah Carey, and proves it several times a night. None of those eccentricities belongs on every song. But who is Chloe to judge? At least those singers assert strong character. At least they're bold. Chloe is a safe singer on the bandstand. She doesn't riff on the Motown and R&B stuff, she doesn't scat or change up the melody on jazz standards. She sings plainly, conservatively, and laughs that Julian has tried so hard for so many years to make her into a jazz singer, when she doesn't have the spirit of improvisation or the pushing of envelopes that it takes to be jazz. As much as she loves it (her favorite album of all time is Miles Davis's *Kind of Blue*), it simply isn't inside of her.

Where Chloe holds her pride is not in the logic-defying feats she can accomplish with her voice, because there are no such feats. She has a limited range at best, not nearly that of most singers she knows. But she uses what she has to great benefit, and rather likes the alto rasp that comes from having sustained polyps on her vocal cords ten years ago, after working a dinner theatre gig, six nights a week, for eight months solid. The high notes will always elude her. But that's okay. She has a warmth and a texture to her voice that she rather likes. And she places her greatest pride on being able to use that texture to interpret a lyric with genuine intimacy. Chloe connects to a song the way an actor connects to a character he is hired to play. She steps inside the shoes and puts the heart of that character on, over her own heart. And it becomes hers for the three-and-a-half-minute duration of the song. This is Chloe's truest gift.

She wonders if this quality belongs to the work Julian has done on honing her over the years. Or if she cultivated this connection to the song on her very own, a by-product of vocal injury that taught her to tap something internal and to appreciate nuance, because she no longer had the goods to be a showboater.

There is such a road weariness that comes with being a musician. Most of them she knows have some malady to complain about. Drummers suffer chronic back pain from lifting their trap cases into their truck beds for years. Piano players battle carpel tunnel in their forearms. Woodwind players are known for TMJ Syndrome in their jaw. Guitar players and electric bass players have extensive chiropractor bills from slinging the straps of their forty-pound instruments over their shoulders. And all a singer has to do to be put out of commission is catch a cold. Voice gone. Of course, every one of them will, before career's end, experience some hearing loss. It's just part of the deal.

And there is never the luxury of being covered by Worker's Compensation, as would a regular person's work-related injuries. Because musicians are independent contractors. There are no benefits, no dental and medical, no 401K's, no paid sick-leave. You want those things, you're on your own, buddy. It's called self-employment, which once upon a time had a certain liberated, I-don't-work-for-THE-MAN cache to it. But today when you say, *"I'm self-employed,"* the response back is usually, *"oooohh, you must really get reamed at tax time."*

Nevertheless, Chloe prefers to look at the hazard margin and the road warts of being a musician as a kind of purposeful design. One that builds a greater character to one's craft than might be found without.

In any case, for however her voice has become seasoned over the long, hard years, it works on this tender ballad that is being played so sparsely by Julian's gifted ensemble that it breaks her heart.

And it has to be breaking Julian's heart, too. She hopes.

One of these days my door will no longer open to the storm outside.
One of these days I'll learn the difference between a widow and a bride.
One of these days.
One of these days.

TRISTAN

It is hot and dry in Hollywood this afternoon. But only a day and a half ago it had rained, so the sky is still clear. Give it one more day. It's already starting to hint again at the yellowing wallpaper of a sky that Hollywood is famous for. For now, a sprinkling of pink storm clouds against radiant blue gives the sky a movie landscape (if fleeting), and screams that there is something profound about to happen. As if the sky is determined to defy the ugly drab of the city it drapes.

Vine Street's storefronts all entice promises of fortune and fame. From music instrument stores to psychics and palm readers. Its restaurants state a bygone glory of old Hollywood legend. *Howard Hughes used to come here with the same anonymous woman for years, every Wednesday, and they sat in that booth RIGHT THERE.* Dilapidated motor lodges. Pawn shops. Stein on Vine. And the tented parking lot of the Musician's Union's Local 47, which has graciously offered to act as host for this momentous tribute to bassist legend, Hayes DeWitt.

The event is officially underway. The tent has somewhat blocked the street noise to give way to an afternoon of music. They can't hear street traffic. But the passing cars can hear the music. And this is how it should be. It might actually beckon pedestrians forth to wonder why and to listen. Maybe even get sucked in.

Tristan listens to Lance Mitchell's group burn through a few classic bop tunes, *Ornithology* for starters. Man, these cats can swing hard! He stands with a Bud Light and feels it deeply inside. And straight-ahead isn't even Tristan's thing. It's just that when it comes to a thing brilliantly executed from a tactile, in-touch, grounded, grab-your-cock standpoint, it kind of just surpasses genre. It's no longer about, *what's your bag, man?* It's ALL your bag. Because it's simply about connection.

He strolls, sips, listens, and shakes hands. He actually likes these kinds of gatherings. Not the reason for it, of course (has Hayes even shown up yet?). But he likes being part of a music "happening," in a room (or tent) with other guys who have lived the life he's lived, and who understand what it is to be compelled. There is a comradeship of struggles. He's already shaken hands with a multitude today. Old friends. Acquaintances. Guys he just gigged with recently, whose faces he recalls, whose playing he definitely recalls but not necessarily their names. He feels nourished by the ritual.

And then suddenly he feels stupored by the overwhelming nature of this moment: The bustling crowd; the live music coming from stadium speakers to his already compromised ears; the applause after each solo, a purely musician tradition; the city around him; the movie studio on the other side of the fence that always begs the curiosity of, *"who's over there being more successful at their careers than I am?"*; the gruff hugs from guys who only ever see each other at gigs or barbecues; the obligation to schmooze. He wanders inside the doors of the union for a minute to stare at the 8x10 Wall-of-Fame, then back out again. He is antsy. And full of thought.

The Local 47 is historic. And like any icon of history, there is controversy and division that follows on its coattails. There is also neglect. All around it is the faded, yellow-stained wallpaper of Hollywood, yet it thrives. Like weeds growing between the cracks of concrete, the union defies all logic and thrives.

Tristan has had a love-hate relationship with the union ever since he first joined as a teenager.

Love, because it was literally his first home in this old whore-tease of a town. 1970. He'd just gotten off the bus (for all he knows, the very same bus that is just now pulling out of the Greyhound station up the street). He stayed at the Elizabeth Hotel on Vine, up toward Hollywood Boulevard. He can't see it from here now, but wonders if it even still reigns as host to homeless teens and runaways, or if it eventually got turned into a Scientology center, as has become the fate of so many other buildings that litter Hollywood.

When he could no longer afford the weekly rents at the Elizabeth, he bunked in a sleeping bag on the lobby floor of the union, and used its restrooms to wash up in, before heading out to pound the pavements every day.

When he realizes that he feels this is the existence Graham should be experiencing, at least for a time, he wonders at his role of parent. We don't want our kids to struggle, to starve, to beg for food. But at the same time, we do want them to feel and appreciate the weight of their pursuits. Tristan can't possibly regret his early days of that very subsistence, of being the hungry artist. It has been crucial in determining the artist he is today. It is the rite of passage, the royal knighting, the Purple Heart that states, "You now have the right to be called a musician."

His son has never experienced this rite of passage. And therefore is still a child. And always will be. Arrested in his development as the artist. This is Tristan's belief.

Does that make him a bad parent?

In the days of sleeping on the union floor, and getting his meals from vending machines, Tristan would lie awake at night, a youth alighting from the nest, about to make his mark on the world, the very best feeling he's ever had in his whole life, and he would marvel with humility and reverence that he was lying within the very hallowed walls (along with all the other hopeful strays) that had made history not even twenty years before that, when in 1953 the Negro Local and the White Local integrated on these very grounds. A movement had amassed, a change had exploded before them, and the stage was being set for a coming decade that would end up being defined as none like it before or since. The result, by the time of those dark-corridored moments in 1970, was that there were still American soldiers over in Viet Nam, the Civil Rights Movement had mobilized not only this nation but nations abroad, King and Malcolm were no longer among the living warriors, and the little deco building on Vine and Gregory in Hollywood, California had carved its own place in the canon of noble radicalism and civil rights history.

And he was a teenager, surrounded by a world of genuine electricity, which was at his feet, and with a life of promise before him.

And then there's the hate. Partly it comes from just being tired and jaded and no longer that wide-eyed teen. But it also comes from a growing bitterness that he pays $160 every year to an organization that has become virtually powerless to uphold the proud union tradition of protecting its workers. Sure, it puts him in their contact book, and he gets a television or sideline job once in a blue moon from it, for which he pays additional work dues.

But the very casual contractors who are his predominant employ virtually ignore the union's limp attempts to enforce fair conditions and wages. And they *can* ignore them, because for every musician who refuses to leave the house for less than $300, there is another waiting in the wings, the true gig whore, or hungry and just off the bus, as he was twenty-five years ago, who is offering to do the same gig for $125.

As long as the community of musicians insists on adhering to the every-man-for-himself creed, and the lot of them refuse to come together to create a movement of solidarity and insistence, the musician's union of Los Angeles will remain what it has become. A ghost.

But then there is today. Every walk of life of them has gathered together to honor one of their own. This is the spirit that first attracted Tristan to music. And it is ironic that this spirit would live (only today, of course) on the very ground that needs it the most. No one here is being paid. They've schlepped all their own equipment. And they're here. For a greater cause than their own aggrandizement.

He doesn't even know the guy who put this thing together. Supposedly this awesome bass player, and one of Hayes's protégés. Tristan originally got the call from Lance, the sax player up on stage right now, blowing on *Impressions*. Apparently this guy throwing the thing had assembled quite a network to help contact all the other musicians. And he did it. The guy pulled it off. Everyone is here. From the everyday cat doing lounge gigs and casuals to the all-star concept bands that only ever attract other musicians to their Baked Potato and Catalina Bar & Grill gigs.

And they are all here to pay tribute to Hayes, and to make music with no compromise. Just as Hayes did it.

He looks over and sees, among the crowd, his employers, Maggie and Andreas Fortune of Fortune Music Events (they actually showed up!). And there's Lester Braddock of Elite Entertainment, another casual office. This guy is truly a head case, Tristan muses, docking musicians a portion of their pay if they're ever caught calling their jobs "casuals" instead of "special events." Tristan shakes his head and rolls his eyes at the absurdity of his industry.

But here they all are, hooting and hollering along with the rest of the crowd. And he wonders if they can even hear the difference in music that isn't about *"getting them up to dance,"* or *"not being too loud"* for the sound ordinance of a particular country club, or *"songs that sound just like the record."* Or music by a band of musicians, one half of which kinda sorta know the tune, the other half of which is divided still again into the ones who know a certain set of chord changes, while the other ones know a different set, creating the ever-calamitous train wreck, and beckoning the wiseacre in the group to yell out, laughing, *"thank you, ladies and gentleman. We ARE Sexual Chocolate!"* a reference to the lame R&B band from an Eddie Murphy movie.

He wonders if the Fortunes or Lester Braddock realize what they've done to music. Maggie Fortune is actually a decent singer, but her husband Andreas has no musical background whatsoever. He's a business man, who started his office when he saw how lucrative hawking his wife's wares for the moneyed contingency of Beverly Hills could be.

He wonders if they can hear what he hears. That there is a difference between playing *Old Time Rock & Roll* just like the record, and taking music to a whole new dimension, even as it is taking you to a new one.

Music is flight.

But the music that is required by the likes of the Fortunes is a stalled car on the freeway, overheated, smelling of bad brakes, tire flattened, battery acid bubbling forth, and hood up, signaling the need for rescue.

At least they've come out to support Hayes. Which is a miracle in itself, because this business is so bipartisan. Musician. Contractor. Ally. Enemy. *Us. Them.*

But this is what a great man does. He unites the divided.

CHLOE

She is one of the boys. In fact, she has striven to fit in for so many years that she cannot even remember when it wasn't so. Even on gigs, when the band adjourns to the break room, it isn't the other singers she gathers with. And there is a separate gathering. Chloe has seen the division of the sexes nowhere more brilliantly illustrated than among musicians.

She credits (or blames) Julian for this phenomenon. Not for the division of the sexes, of course, but for her ambitions to be on the other side. Okay, maybe he is to blame for every misogynistic impulse out there in the world, as well. She laughs, in this absurd fantasy, as she imagines Julian responsible even for the burkas of Middle Eastern women. It is a bitter fantasy. A spiteful one. But for sure, for real, he is responsible for all of her romantic notions about the illustrious Boy's Club.

Julian's line, which woos her ridiculously, vulnerably, gullibly, has always been that she is the exception to her incompetent breed. And instead of wondering what issues this fucked-up guy must have about women, she has instead fed on that "compliment" for years, languishing in the notion that, despite Julian's fundamental disregard for the very group to which she is a member, she is *exceptional*.

It's been so intoxicating to be considered exceptional that she has never even come to the defense of her fellow female singers. Instead, she has taken it upon herself to infiltrate the maleness of this business and to virtually ignore the rest. It isn't her group any longer. And it isn't that she isn't friends with other singers. She actually reveres them in a way she can barely let on, because her agenda precludes being one of them. She is an outsider. She has been converted to a new religion. And fully expects to be seen as merely, sublimely, one of the boys. When the boys laugh at her jokes, the ones the singers never seem to relate to, she feels the pat on the back of inclusion from the ruling class. And she is validated.

The sun pats her on the back today, as she stands in the crowd at the Musician's Union, conflicted. She has never been conscious of this phenomenon until these past crucial hours of assessing the degree of damage in her relationship with Julian.

Is it fair to blame him for her own lack of self-esteem? Especially when she has arrived here today for Hayes's tribute *with* Julian, *still* his girlfriend? Dilemma unfaced? Her man, whose entire life has glided between the raindrops, unconfronted? His neat little meditating, Pottery Barn, Victorian landmark house, *yo cat* universe undisturbed? It's as if she sees it as unfair to put such a burden upon someone so princely and perfect and dirt-free.

Or she is simply a coward.

Today she loathes the way she looks. She loathes the sound of her voice (*too generic, no range*). She loathes her inability to form the kinds of bonds she sees between Gwen and Dominique and Sylvia, who hover together at one little nook, being fellow singers and comrades, laughing and truly enjoying life and each other's company, while Chloe hangs quietly with Julian, or the guys she gigs with, or alone. And she loathes that the pull of Julian is stronger than the pull of her own worth.

She leaves Julian's side (it's the best she'll accomplish today), who's busy, anyway, schmoozing up drummer Bill Fitzmorris, chit-chat chatting, *"when I was out with Miles,"* and chit-chat chatting, *"I'm with Sting now,"* and all the blah, blah, blah, chit-chat, name-dropping bullshit. Ah, the ever-ubiquitous résumé tournament.

It's your volley, honey. He's trumped you with Sting. Can't let him get ahead, now, can we?

She surprises herself with an uncharacteristic sarcasm, and wonders if she can keep the engine revving on it, so that perhaps she'll finally be able to muster the courage to do something.

She walks away to look for Seth and Hayes. She suddenly feels a great haste to find them. Because if she can look in the eyes of her friend who has been close to death and still struggles to surpass it, if she can take his hands in hers and lean in to kiss his cheek, and hug him, and tell him that this is all for him, and that he'd better get better, because the world without Hayes DeWitt is a sadder world, if she can remind herself what is truly important, and that petty observations about her boyfriend do not fit the category, then perhaps she can shake off this sick narcissism and remember what everyone at this gathering has been put on this earth to do. Including her.

A big hug comes from Tristan Baylor, instead, in the midst of her search for the guest of honor.

"Hey, girl. How's it goin'?"

"Hey, you."

"Can you believe this thing?"

"I know. This is huge. Am I seeing things, or is this being broadcast? Did you see all those boom operators?"

"Yeah, I think KLON's doin' a live feed. Apparently they're doin', like, radio pledges and the whole bit."

"Oh my God, I can't believe Seth pulled that off. That's awesome."

"Yeah, that's the guy puttin' this thing on, right? I don't know him."

"Oh, you're kidding. He's great. You two would totally hit it off. I was actually just on my way looking for him and Hayes."

"I haven't seen Hayes yet. Hey, how's he doin' anyway? Is

he even up to makin' somethin' like this?"

"Well, it's not like he's bedridden or anything. But it is supposed to be a surprise, so gettin' him outta the house might be a chore. Latest I know is that he probably needs a second new heart. And you know how long he waited for the first one. Not to mention his age is a factor, and blah, blah, blah."

"Jesus Christ. Does it ever end?"

"Apparently not."

"This is what you and I get to look forward to."

"Mmmmm."

They are sobered by a moment of poignant reality, followed by an awkward silence and a heavy heart.

"So, is Julian here? You guys performing today?"

And there it is. Would Tristan have even bothered to come hug her and chat her up if Julian Troupe wasn't her other half? As ridiculous and paranoid as it all seems, she cannot shake the compulsion to assign a culprit to everything that is wrong with her life.

But Tristan is a dear friend, who has never been duplicitous with her. What the Hell is she thinking?

"Yeah, he's here. Actually, it's more like, Julian's performing and I'm just sort of tagging along and being allowed the privilege of sitting in."

"Wait a minute. I thought *he* was doin' *your* project."

"He is. I mean, but…it's his band. All his guys are playin' on the record. I didn't get to pick anybody. And, you know, he's still got his thing, 'Julian Troupe and Lazarus,' so they're mainly doin' stuff from their record today, and then, just like, one or two of mine. You know, like, '…*and featuring…*'"

"Uh oh. Do I detect some trouble in paradise?"

"No, no, no, I'm just…I'm just in a mood. Hey, but if you ever need a female voice in your project, I mean, I know you've got the Indian chanter, or whatever you call that, but you've also got background vocals, I noticed, and, man, I am absolutely in love with your album."

"Oh, you finally gotta chance to listen to it?" he offers excitedly.

"Oh my God, Tristan, I have listened to your album to death ever since you gave it to me."

"Wow. That means the world to me."

"And I am not just blowin' smoke. I mean, you know how it is. Every musician and his brother has a CD out. I've been handed a million CDs from friends on gigs. Most of which I've played maybe once, and then never listen to again. I mean, cuz they just all start to sound the same after awhile."

"Yeah, you know what I do when somebody hands me their CD?" Tristan leans in to confide. "I open up the shrink wrap, toss the fuckin' disc in the trash can, and use the case as a coaster, thank you very fuckin' much."

Chloe laughs a laugh that truly lifts her, if only for a moment, from the anvil on her chest. This dark cynicism feeds her. It is the very code of inclusion she knows they don't share with the other singers. She often feigns this dark cynicism herself. But Chloe is too wide-eyed, too hopeful, to be a true cynic.

"But yours," she continues, "I'm tellin' you, it stands out from the same ol' shit. Man, I would be honored, if you ever needed a singer on your project."

"Well, you should sit in with us today. I mean, I know you're doin' your thing with Julian, but, you know, if you feel in the mood, jump on up there with us. I'm doin' one of Hayes's tunes today that I arranged for the band, but otherwise it's everything off the album. I mean, Julian wouldn't care, right?"

"Julian is not my babysitter," she says defensively, but tastes the bitter sorghum of a lie on her tongue.

"Ow!"

"No, I'm just kidding. Everything's fine with us. But I swear to God, Tristan, I know your tunes. If you dare me, I will get up there with you," she offers with a playful threat.

"Good. Well then, I dare you. Man, it'd be a blast. So, how is your CD comin' along, anyway?"

"Well, I'm absolutely in love with it. I mean, Julian has done this really remarkable job with the tracks. Like, my songs, they sound so much better than they actually are. It's amazing what real musicians can do to bring a song alive."

"I don't wanna hear it. You are a real musician."

"No, but you know what I mean."

And yet she eats it up, all the while fully conscious of the demon sugar.

"I think I'm a decent enough songwriter. But I'm not a player. My piano skills are just marginal enough to compose without the aid of a co-writer. But then a real player suddenly plays my chart down, and it's, like, 'Jesus Christ, where did that come from? Is that MY song?' And I'm, like, 'hey, I wrote that!'"

She laughs. She could never see herself having this conversation with another singer, which bothers her. It certainly isn't because she feels superior to them. She actually feels quite small in their presence, because they have a sisterhood, of which she is not a part, all because of a little, deeply embedded hardwiring called Julian Troupe.

"So, how's Graham?" she asks, climbing once again out of her insistent narcissism.

"He's good. He's uh, um..." Tristan looks as if he's just lost his train of thought, perhaps distracted by the introduction of the next act and the welcoming applause.

"He's, um, he just got a record deal."

"What! Oh my God, Tristan, are you kidding!"

"No," he offers, "he's, he's pretty ecstatic. He's got this sort of heavy-metal rap thing goin'—"

"Yeah, no, I remember us talkin' about it—"

"—He's pretty good, I gotta say."

"Oh my God, that's awesome. I remember when Graham was just a little boy," she skirls with a whiny baby talk that only women are famous for. "God, have we known each other that long? And you know, believe me, I know how much Papa Baylor hates his son becoming a rapper. But some of it can actually be pretty interesting. I mean, if he doesn't just go down that same old tired *bitches and hoes* road that everybody else seems to."

"Yeah, no, I agree. I think he's got a real shot at bein' somethin' special."

"Well, I'm so happy for him. And for you too, proud Papa."

Chloe hugs Tristan as though the good news is of his own record deal. Because, it's all the same, isn't it? The successes of the child also belong to the parent. She looks in his eyes and sees his happiness. Graham's lucky to have Tristan as a father and mentor.

She wishes she could feel as heart-warmed about her own mentor. And suddenly she is envious of Graham. Not of his good news, but that his father brags of him when he's not present. She wonders if Julian ever speaks of her as highly when she's not in a room.

She is overtaken by a sudden suspicion that the world is conspiring to give her no props. That it intends to exclude her. And this fear irks her for being insane and irrational, when her ego has always lain in her ultra togetherness.

"And, oh, by the way, how'd that gig go last night?" Tristan asks. "Man, you called me yesterday morning in a panic. I assume you found somebody."

"Aagghh. Long story. Boring. Let's just say I survived it, and I'm still standing."

"Yeah, well, sounds like mine last night. It's the age-old moan."

"Exactly."

"It's kind of like *ohm*, you know? The universal vibration

they use in Eastern meditation? You could say that *moan* is the musician's *ohm*."

He puts each thumb and index finger together, closes his eyes, and sings in monotone, *"I - hate - my - fuck - ing - gig - I - hate - my - fuck - ing - life - moooaaaannnnn."*

Chloe laughs. And is suddenly reminded of the multiple phone messages left on her voicemail this morning from DeVoe. For the time being, at least, she has decided to be as wounded as DeVoe had been. She certainly has more reason. Why isn't it as easy to shake Julian off?

"Well, I think we're up next," she says. "I should probably get back stage and see what's goin' on."

"Go get 'em, girl."

Go get 'em, girl.

Those four words. If only Tristan knew just how much they meant to Chloe. It is validation far more valid than any Julian has ever deigned to pass her way.

"Thanks, Tristan."

Chloe moves through the crowd, speaking to several folks on her way to the side of the stage, including hugs and kisses to her fellow singers. She locates Julian and watches Dorothy Favor on stage. Dorothy exudes a grand pathos, coming from someplace very deep and real. And is someone Chloe has always been riveted by. Never met her. Has just heard about her and has listened to her for years. Chloe figures she's never met this local legend because Dorothy's probably too old to be hired for casuals anymore. Maybe in her sixties? Chloe guesses. Because the cruel reality is that old guys on a casual is not the end of the world. But old gals?

Dorothy's younger ex-husband, Nick Brandt, is Chloe's favorite piano player in this town. He and Chloe did a six-month stint together at the Smokehouse in Toluca Lake years ago. It was one of the best gigs Chloe's ever had. In fact, Nick is who Chloe wanted to play on her CD, but Julian had other ideas. Nick Brandt would've taken it someplace else, for sure. They are dear friends. But Chloe also knows that Dorothy Favor (and not she) is Nick's favorite singer in this town. What she wouldn't give to have that kind of reverence from Julian.

Dorothy dedicates *Spring Can Really Hang You Up the Most* to Hayes over the microphone, and then sings it with a tenderness that breaks Chloe's heart, the kind of singing the masses just don't appreciate anymore. Chloe makes note that she now sounds just like every other bitter musician she knows. Is it just an act? Another ploy to be one of the boys? To merit entree into The Club? Or does she truly feel this? Either way is a little bit of a depressing notion.

She looks around and sees her world, the world of music-makers. It is as divided a world as it is unified, between musicians and contractors, singers and players, *yo cats* and casual grunts. She even thinks about Tristan's son, Graham, who's just been handed the opportunity of a lifetime, an opportunity everyone under this tent today would kill for, and if the kid's smart he'll take with him into the land of stardom some of his father's wisdom on what it is to truly love music and to work hard for it. And she thinks about DeVoe, her non-working musician ex-friend, who makes music purely for the joy of making it, and therefore has no clue what it takes to do business and be professional. In many ways, as much as that has irked her over this past twenty-four hours, it makes him kind of free. Free from the burdens of being a gig whore, a road hog, a pavement pounder, a hustler, a schmoozer; all the things that she and her kind must be to survive in this town.

She looks up and sees the Hollywood sign, almost obscured by the developing smog, though the day had started off clear from the rains two days ago. This is where they come. All the hopefuls. Unless it's Nashville. Maybe Vegas. Maybe New York. But this is where everyone is told they can become a star. And what the Hell does that mean, anyway? All she's ever wanted was enough recognition to be able to keep making music on her own terms.

I guess THAT'S what it means.

As she looks around at an assemblage of L.A.'s best, she wonders if any of them are still hoping, or if they've all just settled.

The applause for Dorothy Favor's finale jolts Chloe out of her reverie, and the pumped-in music that's meant to play between acts spits right out. It's all Hayes DeWitt recordings. Nice touch.

One set of players starts to tear down their equipment, as another set floods the stage with theirs. The exchange is respectful but slightly chaotic. Backline has been provided, so Julian's drummer only has to provide his own cymbals and his bass pedal. The bass player plugs in his pick-up, the keyboard player messes around with knobs, music stands are bumped around, cords and cables go snaking across the stage, with the crew bounding around just trying to make everything run smoothly, monitors are re-directed, and the crowd beyond the scrim has, for the time being, turned their attentions away and onto each other, schmoozing, networking, shaking hands, passing out business cards, or fliers for their next gig, doing what is essentially the Musician's Virginia Reel, all with beers and plates of food in their hands, before it's time again to pay attention to the act on stage.

Before Chloe knows it, she is that act, with Julian beside her, guitar strapped on, the rest of Lazarus in place, and the announcer giving the crowd, "and now ladies and gentlemen, JULIAN TROUPE...AND LAZARUS!"

The crowd goes nuts, and Lazarus socks the audience's chest with a tune of Chloe's that Julian arranged and turned from a tepid little bossa nova into a poly-rhythmic, time-signature-change-every-other-measure, Brecker-esque opus that Chloe has to count furiously in her head just to sing the freaking thing correctly, even though it's her tune. When that much is going on in Chloe's head, there's no real way to disappear into the song. It all just becomes an illustration in technical wizardry and flash, but no real soul. This is not one of Chloe's favorites from her upcoming album, though every musician she knows will be impressed with it. But it's not like the gentle waltz ballad that stayed in her head all of last night and this morning. The one she would've preferred they opened with.

Chloe holds on tight, sings her ass off, hitting every mark, and wows the crowd, even if she isn't wowing herself. But it isn't only counting that's burdening Chloe's head. It's also how the announcer introduced them. She didn't even merit her name being in the introduction, and she's the one Seth called for this, not Julian. Like everything else, Julian takes over and makes it his. This is *her* up here singing, *her* song, which is about to come out on *her* album, but the crowd has been introduced to Julian Troupe and Lazarus.

She also thinks about Hayes. See, this is what happens when she can't disappear into a song. A whole other grocery list of concerns flood her thoughts, instead. Why didn't she remember to buy a bouquet of flowers so that she could make a grand gesture of handing them to Hayes when she was done with her set? Something for the whole world to see her do, a gesture always thought of by women, a tradition that does lift them up from the pragmatic natures of men. Yet she didn't think to do it.

And when she's done, she simply walks off the stage during a furious applause, as she hears Julian say over the mic, "Ladies and gentlemen, that was the lovely Chloe Baptiste, singing a song from her upcoming CD, *Folklore*. Please look for it." He doesn't say that she wrote it, because he kind of considers it his song now. He doesn't beckon her back for one more, like maybe for the pretty waltz that she would've dedicated to Hayes. Instead, he gets on with Lazarus's repertoire as quickly as he can. As quickly as Chloe has walked away.

There is a gulf between Chloe Baptiste and Julian Troupe. It's been there all along. But not truly felt by Chloe with such grandly dismissive impact until this very minute. She admits she's been a little slow to catch on.

There's a Pavilions just down the street. She is done with Julian. And she is off to find flowers for Hayes.

SETH

They have been this way for hours.

Seth looks at the clock on the nightstand, but has ceased (maybe an hour or two ago) wondering what is going on in Hollywood. Earlier the questions raced in a panic: Is the thing moving forward without them? Is anyone even aware that the guest of honor isn't there, yet? Or are they all just waiting around quietly, like bored stags at a prom, and flies gathering around the food?

Those questions are gone now. There is only this space. Seth wishes it were a more profound space. If it must happen now, this threat, this morbid inkling that Hayes dances in front of him, then why can't it be more extraordinary a surrounding, something befitting a great novel? Something with flowers in a nearby meadow, abundant enough to smell, a great closing metaphor for a full life? Or the ocean hum just outside a window that travels one's life-tales in its whistles, and emits images of introspective Bergman films with diffused light? Or a bird on a windowsill that gives a dying man his last brilliant imagery?

Why, instead, are the ochre Granada Hills walls duller than usual, the window vertical blinds dirty and allowing in little of the daylight, the faint sound of a lawnmower somewhere in the neighborhood, and the robe that Hayes sleeps in almost melting into him, unfresh?

Why isn't death more beautiful, as it is in movies? Something not to fear, but like a great Zen warrior is passed through with resolve and wisdom and grace?

Seth isn't sure he is the man for this job. But he shoves unsure aside. If he thinks too much, he'll be out the door, running with his tail between his legs.

He holds Hayes's hands tightly *(don't loosen that grip even a little, or you're out that door)* as Hayes floats in and out of consciousness, at times speaking to Seth as though Seth is his son or his wife, the son and wife who walked away years ago. That's new.

"Hand me my bow," Hayes whispers, slicing the silence in two.

His eyes have been closed for awhile now, but he doesn't sleep. And Seth can't quite make out the request, because Hayes is muttering and has lost his ability for clear, concise speech. Seth stares into the face that has stopped looking back.

"Hand me, hand me my, my, my…"

Hayes is frustrated that simple words don't come to him. What was he just asking for a second ago? *The goddamned meds!*

"My, my, my, the, the, the…"

He still has possessive pronouns. He takes furious mental note of every word that remains useful to him.

Seth watches him, brow furrowed in an effort to decipher the code. Did he just say his bow?

Then he knows for sure, as Hayes begins to "play" his arco bass. The delirium is deep today. Seth watches Hayes's old hands, which suddenly seem ancient. They move deliberately in the air, even as his eyes remain closed. Wait, no, he isn't playing it. Seth studies the mimed gesture that has more belief in it than any genius Marcel Marceau. The art of mime always teaches that you inhabit your belief in the objects that are not really there. They ARE really there, if there is to be brilliance.

Hayes is shimmering today in his dementia.

He is giving the bow some rosin. His left hand, trembling from the drugs, cups the rosin in his palm, while the right one drags the bow across it. It is almost beautiful, this other reality, this tiny pocket of the past in Hayes's hands. He hasn't literally touched his contrabass in months, but now he prepares his bow. Seth sees the bow's fibers bury themselves in the lip of the indented rosin and slide across. It is sensuous, this tactile connection of textures and smells. He can even smell the rosin. This goes on for some minutes, as Hayes then abandons the rosin and raises his left arm higher than he should, to "grip" the bass' neck. He starts to hum, but it is more of an indecipherable set of grunts and growls.

Hayes's throat is scratchy, and soon the need for a glass of water follows a coughing fit. His hands suddenly flail about in his fit. If he'd actually been playing, he'd've dropped the invaluable 1726 German bass to the ground, but Seth is faster and "catches" it for him.

Seth then scurries quickly to the kitchen for a glass of water, and returns to find Hayes deeply again immersed in images and anchors of the past. His head tilts to the side, resting on the neck of the bass, looking like some tilted-headed portrait of Madonna and Child.

This is too much. Seth is ready to throw twenty years to the winds. It would be so easy. One swift move to the front door, and this moment that is almost breaking him is no longer witnessed. And Hayes would never even know. He belongs to the dementia.

Seth falls. His composure has been iron. His last shed tear was when his father died, a man he hated, yet cried for him. Before that, easily, as a child. Perhaps a scraped knee. No. It was when his boyhood dog died. Seth simply doesn't cry. It isn't in his DNA. Some people just can't.

His body isn't even sure it knows how, and so it shakes and rattles indiscriminately, while his chest heaves and his face swells with an unbearable heat. His crying is almost coughing. He cannot stand by and watch this.

"I was thinking the Koussevitzky might've been nice," Hayes says, as he bows his bass, the one that in reality sits in a corner, covered in its canvass, a few yards away. "But it's been so long, I don't know if I remember the repertoire well enough. But I have been shedding these cello suites, transposed down to accommodate the bass. Here, tell me how this sounds. I'm not positive it translates well. You know what I mean. And if anyone tells you otherwise, they're full of shit. Key centers do have characters and emotions all their own, with pieces sometimes inspiring the greatest cries in one key, while not sparking a damned thing in another."

Seth is the one who's been shedding the Bach Cello Suites lately. A fact he'd shared with Hayes only a few weeks ago, but Hayes barely paid attention. He'd also shared that very phenomenon about key centers having their own emotions to Hayes. But most things about Seth's little projects outside of the projects for Hayes, Hayes has simply never given much time to. Seth telling Hayes that he's shedding the Bach in keys conducive to the bass, like many things, simply goes in one ear and out the other.

Now this.

Seth realizes it is only pockets of memory, unconnected, just spilling out in random order. But he also now sees that nothing goes in one ear and out the other. Hayes simply picks and chooses, fussily, what he does and doesn't have time for. But is actually storing every bit of it away for future use.

"I can't hear it!" Hayes suddenly cries out in delirium. "Why can't I hear it?"

Hayes's hands flail more furiously about now. His heart shouldn't be affording this much movement.

Seth's own heart races. What can he do? He looks over in the direction of the German, in the corner covered. Hayes's baby. His pride. Which has a pedigree. It was once owned and performed on by the principle bassist in Haydn's orchestra.

Joseph-freaking-Haydn! No one touches this bass. Seth never has. In twenty years, Seth has never touched the German.

As Hayes's dementia threatens to give his imagined concert away, and perhaps spark a panic of, *"I never wanted to go out this way, stupid and drooling and rolling around in my own shit!"* Seth approaches the German, lifting the canvassed cover from it gingerly. It is a monster. Much larger than his own modern upright. And Seth is a taller man than Hayes. He can't even imagine Hayes playing this thing, as he holds its broad neck in his grip. He lifts the weighty thing delicately, just a few inches off the floor and brings it closer to Hayes's bedside.

"Why can't I hear it? Is my hearing going? That can't happen! How can I gig if my hearing goes!"

Seth pulls up Hayes's gig stool, but is careful to keep out of Hayes's sightlines. He brings the bass near him, drawing its neck to his left shoulder, picks up the bow, and plays. *Will this work?*

The instant that the Prelude beckons forth, Hayes is calmed, like a hypnosis patient suddenly clapped out of his hysteria. *Wow. Can it really be that simple?* Hayes resumes his own playing, and smiles to hear the results coming back at him beautifully. This alone is enough to please Seth, who has never felt that Hayes really believed in his playing. That he isn't yelling, *"God, I sound like crap!"* means Hayes approves, even if he does believe it's his own hands making this music.

It is deep and rich. Not only the execution, but the composition. It is the No. 5 Prelude of the Cello Suites. And Hayes chose it. Even in his warbled humming, Seth was able to recognize it. It is a prelude that opens with a gust, only to then sink back into submission with a fragility Hayes has never been known for, but which seems to spell his life today. It is, therefore, the piece of his choosing, the piece that speaks to him, for a reason. Not the Koussevitzky, with its sforzando bravado, really much more apropos of Hayes's character. But the Bach. A diametrically opposed poetry. A sentimental cadence from an unsentimental grouch.

Seth plays it delicately and stares at Hayes.

As long as Hayes plays, so will Seth.

At this point, what will anything matter if Seth spills a few stupid tears on the wood of the German? He can't quell his weeping. He fights with his twisted face to keep it from distorting in complete collapse, but to no use.

And then Hayes stops. He is tired. It takes strength to hold something as grand as the German. He played it in the L.A. Philharmonic once, under Zubin Mehta. He was a sub for a friend. He loves to tell that story.

Maybe this is where he was, Seth thinks. He stops, too. He watches Hayes cautiously and pulls away from the German, this icon he was never to touch, and is full. Full with conflict and fear.

He places the bass back in its corner, making sure not to disrupt wherever Hayes is. He quietly tiptoes back to Hayes's bedside and sits with him. As they began the day, so they are here again.

Hayes's breathing is fitful. He's just run a marathon. Just played under Zubin Mehta. Seth is exhausted, too. He leans his head down onto Hayes's hands, which he has gripped with his own. It is, by far, the most forward physical gesture Seth has ever made. These two men do not even hug. But he is close to collapse, and Hayes is elsewhere. It doesn't really matter where Seth lays his head.

After some minutes of Hayes having fallen asleep (precious minutes for Seth, minutes that do not require his dire focus and keen judgment), Hayes awakens again, slips one of his hands out from under Seth's buried face, and places it on Seth's head.

Seth feels it. His lungs tighten in a silent gasp. Is this forbidden? This intimacy into which they've never ventured before? This intimacy is not one of student and teacher, not fellow musicians. They are father and son. But father and son without the strangling binds of dysfunction. It is territory strange for both men.

"I'm sorry," Hayes whispers.

The silence screams all around his utterance in a tornadoed flurry.

"I'm sorry I failed you as a father."

Wraps around it like streams of papyrus.

Seth's brow raises, pulse speeds, ears prick, even as his face remains buried. Hayes speaks softly. Vaguely straddling *here* and *there*.

"If you can't forgive my weakness as a man...as a father...which I have no real right to ask...at least...at least, don't let it stain you. Don't let it send you out into the world skittish and untrusting. Intolerant of intimacy. Afraid of everything and everyone. Let my begging of your forgiveness tell you how I have loved you, in a way I could never do with arms of embrace, or words, or even my listening ear. I was afraid. But of what? In the end, we all come to this moment. We all pass through the door. We relinquish our worldly attachments and our ego, and say goodbye to those who have loved us. We take with us only our sentience. So, really, what on earth is there to fear? It's so foolish! That, what? That if we love too much, it'll turn around and bite us? It never does. It NEVER does. So, why do so many fathers fuck up their sons?"

Seth's eyes are squeezed shut. His grip, white-knuckled and fisting, clings to covers and blankets now, on either side of Hayes's resting frame, as Hayes's hands crown Seth's head. These words that Seth has imagined for years, endlessly, obsessively, conjured in an almost autistic loop, suddenly pour into his ears. And he spills a coughing-fit cry, a dank, sobbing, guttural weeping. He cries until his chest is on fire. Until his eyes are swollen shut. And the clock advances. And Hayes has no more words. Seth cries until he passes into a kind of complete shutdown slumber. The first of its depth that he has experienced in many long months.

When he wakes — not sure how long, but it is dark out — Hayes is gone.

Seth lifts his head, but even before lifting it, feels death beneath him. He knows before he even looks in Hayes's face. When he does, the eyes are closed, the mouth seemingly at peace. There is nothing to adjust, as he's seen in movies. No eyelids to close. No gaping mask of death to correct.

Seth stares. No more tears come. He's out of tears. There is only the merciless silence and his own rattled lungs pumping air through swollen nostrils.

The full first moment of knowledge is nothing Seth has ever experienced before. It is an unwieldy standing still of time, a shaky movement of space, a piercing shriek of feedback, the way sound bounces and rounds onto itself. The room is still. Not even the earlier breeze that wrestled the verticals to tinkling is present. The air, and the walls, and the curtains, and the bedspread that wraps death within it, are as still as the heart that has stopped beating, as the breath that no longer passes through the body.

He sits in the quiet. Is even comforted by it, somewhat. He knows he should get up and move. Call the Neptune Society (Hayes had made arrangements with them more than a year ago). Try to get a family member on the phone. Something. But he can't.

All he can accomplish, as he sits and stares, hands helplessly by his sides, is a replay of Hayes's words, a set of words that will never cease their brilliant burdening for the remainder of Seth Robb's life.

The question that plagues is this: Was Hayes speaking to his own son, believing Seth to be him? And if so, then there is a deeply intimate gratification Seth feels that he would be the one chosen to be the conduit Hayes needed. To be allowed the great honor of giving Hayes that moment.

Or was Hayes doing something even more extraordinary? Something that, in this instant, races and pounds at Seth's heart and trembling breath? Especially because it is a moment that should be used to set one's own house in order. Was Hayes giving Seth the crucial goodbye Seth's own father had never managed? The goodbye that would've freed Seth, all of these years, to opt for peace?

He cries again (he was wrong about being emptied of all tears) and will never know the answer. It will go buried, along with all the future music Hayes DeWitt had yet to compose, where so many shimmering gems retire.

And suddenly Seth finds himself upon his epiphany. That one we each get our shot at, once in our lifetime, if we're lucky enough to be paying attention. It is an epiphany Seth prays Hayes can hear him loudly assert from wherever Hayes has gone to: That whichever of the two revelations is true, either one defiantly rejects Hayes's earlier claim that he had never, in this life, done that one great thing.

Somewhere in this city tonight someone is playing a bar mitzvah.

Somewhere else someone is facing a nightmare load-in at a star-studded, rooftop, poolside party, for a four-hour continuous.

Somewhere there's a jazz gig going on in a tiny club, where every musician in town, who isn't gigging, will converge to see their favorite guitar player shed stupefying chops on his axe.

Somewhere a lone pianist plays his bouncy show tunes for high-end department store shoppers.

Somewhere a drummer is being hassled by hotel security for blocking the loading dock as he tries to unload his two-hundred pounds of equipment for a debutante ball.

Somewhere a trumpet-playing busker blasts out his cracked Miles repertoire on a street corner, for a coffee tin of change.

Somewhere a singer is excitedly preparing to go out on her first major tour with the highest-paid recording star in the industry, and have her life changed forever.

Somewhere the singer who didn't get that same job shows up to her lounge gig, where she fends off drunken lechers, who slobber requests, while waiving obnoxious twenties in her face, which they attempt to shove into her cleavage.

Somewhere a garage band debuts their set at a trendy rock club to celebrate the release of their new indie CD and their upcoming European tour.

Somewhere there are contracts being signed for record deals that promise the world to young punks who are about to make a splash.

Somewhere are the elder statesmen of those young punks, unemployed on this Sunday evening, who've either already made their splash, or are trudging along, just making meager ends meet by the elusive and alluring means of music.

This is the city for such a tapestry.

And on Vine Street, a community of many have gathered to celebrate one of their own, who has left them behind, but not untouched.

Cyril Brandt has just finished his last number, with brother Emil on drums and Walter Reddick on bass, and wonders where his youngest brother is. Nick should be here, Cyril notes with some irritation. Nick did, after all, head the celebrated quartet that once contained Hayes on bass, Balthazar Brava on drums, and Nick's ex, Dorothy Favor, a formidable vocalist, who sang earlier.

Fucking Nick!

Raz Emery is not far away, telling a story to a circle of guys about the assholes (he calls his fellow players with adoration) who pranked him on the bandstand a few nights ago, by lowering his drum throne to about a foot from the ground and raising his high-hat to tower above him, so that when they all came back from their set break, and had to immediately go into a *hora*, there he was in the most absurd squat, reaching to the sky to hit his high-hat, because he had no time to change it all back. Everyone on the bandstand was fallen out in laughing hysterics (except for the leader, of course, whose job it is to be unnecessarily nervous).

"But that's alright. I got the bass player back by pluckin' out an Ab on the piano when he asked me for an A to tune his bass. That mother-fucker starts *Hava Nagila*, LOUDLY, in the wrong fuckin' key! You have never seen such horror on a face in your life. It was beautiful. And these fuckin' clients never have a clue. Man, I have so much fun up there with those cut-ups. You gotta, just to keep sane, you know?"

Lance Mitchell gives an impromptu tour of the inside of the Union to his wife and kids. He hopes someday to pass the love he has for music to his children.

"You don't have to choose it for a living, kids. In fact, I'm not so sure I would recommend it." He and his wife laugh at a joke the kids are not wise to. "But if you can find a connection to music, you'll discover that everything else in your life simply has a richer color to it."

His son and daughter listen intently. They are young and wide-eyed still. Just give them time.

Lavery Snow stops by for a literal minute, to add his celebrity to the cause. And is off again, within an instant, to go wherever it is that celebrities go.

Seth Robb walks up, having just marched a hundred miles back from the war, wounded, shell-shocked, but alive.

It is hours now since Hayes took his last breath. And in that time, so many immediate particulars had to be taken care of. Once Hayes was taken away by the Neptune Society (Seth will have the chore, or the privilege, to decide what to do with his ashes), Seth got the Hell out of the Granada Hills house as quickly as his truck would drive him, and found himself here.

As he walks up, numb, but in need of a balm that only this tribute to Hayes can give him, he stands in the back, uninterested in being noticed. He is overtaken by how many have shown. This is breathtaking, he notes, as he looks out over the vista.

He witnesses such a reverence given to this proceeding that he wonders if they can sense that Hayes is gone. And if they do know, then there is a weird kind of comfort in the notion that they continue in the celebration of this man's life, anyway. Because it is a celebration of the immortal living organism of music. An excuse (is there a better one?) to commune for the simple sake of it.

But he realizes that he is asking a more spiritual serendipity of his cohorts than is probably the reality. More likely, everyone here expects to see their old friend again.

To laugh with him and exchange musician jokes. Old self-deprecating standbys like:

"Mommy, when I *grow up*, I want to be a *musician*. Well, honey, you know you can't do both."

BA-*DUM*-BUMP!

And to make music with him again, and to see him in action, an artist to behold.

Eventually Seth will have to be the one to let his community know that musician and composer Hayes DeWitt has died today. But until that moment, he plans to watch this celebration as Hayes would have.

A tender acoustic guitar is presently being played by Tristan Baylor, a beautifully strummed take on Hayes's famed composition, *Gilead* (the reference is to a biblical city that bears trees which render a healing balm). Gilead is a healing piece. Hayes's best, Seth feels. Apparently so do others, since it's been recorded by everyone from Wynton Marsalis to Oscar Peterson.

Seth doesn't know anyone in Tristan's band, but the drummer hits his snare with a kitchen pot top, which Seth is intrigued by. The bass player lays down a pocket with a round, velvety sound and a solid feel. A violinist counters the melody with poignant lines. And an Indian chanter, a tiny elderly woman, provides a true haunting to Hayes's most spiritual composition to date. Of course, Seth fully expects Hayes to keep composing from the Great Irascible Musician Beyond.

Standing next to the Indian wailer is Seth's friend, Chloe Baptiste. He's only just noticed her. Wasn't she supposed to perform with Julian today?

She has joined in with a blatantly apparent euphoria, and improvises counter lines of oohh's and aahh's to the chanter's powerful ragas. It seems so out of Chloe's character, Seth thinks, to attempt something so bold and naked against a music system that is viewed by the educated with a kind of reverence. Chloe's never been known to expose herself too often to the scrutiny of her peers. She's actually a very safe singer, and somewhat shy.

But here she stands today, with Tristan Baylor's band, not out front, just one in the fabric, as Tristan sings the lead with a poignantly wrecked tenor voice.

Gilead is an instrumental piece, but Tristan (Seth assumes) has penned a beautiful set of lyrics and a rootsy, bluesy, Eastern, eclectic arrangement of Hayes's famous jazz anthem.

That is the true beauty of music, Seth asserts, smiling.

It belongs to everyone.

He notices a bushel of fresh irises in Chloe's left hand as she sings. He doesn't usually give flowers much thought, but notices the dainty purple wonders tonight because he guesses they are intended for Hayes.

His throat gets caught just a tiny bit more with each thought of his mentor, his friend, and tonight, he has boldly claimed, his father.

As Tristan's band comes to the close of Hayes DeWitt's *Gilead*, Tristan leans again into the mic and speaks over the din of applause.

"For Hayes. You'll be back on that bass in no time, buddy."

To which Chloe and the rest on stage, as well as the adoring audience, hoot and whistle and cheer.

Seth falls again unexpectedly. *Fucking tears.* He has many more left in him than he could possibly know at this moment.

It will be a lovely, gradual discovery.

Gilead lives across town, as well, in a little bar on Eighth Street in the downtown district of L.A.

Nick Brandt couldn't make it to the tribute today, or remain sober, despite repeated promises to Otto, his friend and ally at the Orchid Club.

Though he knows he shouldn't, he is waiting for Dorothy. *Hayes'll understand.*

He sits at the lonely piano on this moonless night, unable to part from it, and continues for the two or three stragglers who begin to pay attention to him from their tables and at the bar.

"Everybody raise your glasses...and help me salute a dear friend, who's done everything in this life from Carnegie Hall to Casualties. Cuz that's just what the job is, man. But his music will last long after every one of us is gone. Because he is one o' the greats. And the greats are never forgotten."

He starts in on *Gilead*, a delicate, introspective rendering that only Nick Brandt's fingers can accomplish with such artful irony. A few tears accompany, but otherwise it is unadorned and sparse.

"This one's for Hayes."

And from far away, though they are merely feet from him, and though there are but a few, Nick hears the unearthly clinking together of a hundred glasses.

OTHER WORKS BY ANGELA CAROLE BROWN

BOOKS
The Assassination of Gabriel Champion
The Kidney Journals: Memoirs of a Desperate Lifesaver

BLOGS
Bindi Girl Chronicles

ALBUMS
The Slow Club
Resting on the Rock
Expressionism
Music for the Weeping Woman
Winter
Global Yoga